Reign
of the SEVEN
SPELLBLADES

XIII

Bokuto Uno

ILLUSTRATION BY
Ruria Miyuki

Guy Greenwood

Annie Mackley

Pete Reston

"You've got a lotta nerve. You survived that mess through sheer luck, and a minute later, you're trying to poach him?"

Ursule Valois

"...Loosely, yes? I thiiink I see the concept of your tea party."

"Oh, is that an epiphany?"

Nanao Hibiya

Oliver Horn

Michela McFarlane

Katie Aalto

"Y'all are gloomy as hell. None of you are even trying to hide that something happened."

CONTENTS

Prologue —————————————— 001

Chapter 1 Separation ————— 007

Chapter 2 Opportunity ———— 037

Chapter 3 Tear —————————— 091

Chapter 4 Dissent ——————— 141

Epilogue ——————————————— 185

Reign of the Seven Spellblades
Bokuto Uno

Reign of the SEVEN SPELLBLADES

XIII

Bokuto Uno

ILLUSTRATION BY
Ruria Miyuki

YEN ON

New York

Reign of the Seven Spellblades, Vol. 13
Bokuto Uno

Translation by Andrew Cunningham
Cover art by Ruria Miyuki

NANATSU NO MAKEN GA SHIHAISURU Vol. 13
©Bokuto Uno 2023
Edited by Dengeki Bunko
First published in Japan in 2023 by KADOKAWA CORPORATION, Tokyo.
English translation rights arranged with KADOKAWA CORPORATION, Tokyo
through TUTTLE-MORI AGENCY, INC., Tokyo.

English translation © 2025 by Yen Press, LLC

Yen On
150 West 30th Street, 6th Floor
New York, NY 10001

Visit us at yenpress.com
facebook.com/yenpress
twitter.com/yenpress
yenpress.tumblr.com
instagram.com/yenpress

First Yen On Edition: June 2025
Edited by Yen On Editorial: Rachel Mimms
Designed by Yen Press Design: Jane Sohn, Andy Swist

Yen On is an imprint of Yen Press, LLC.
The Yen On name and logo are trademarks of Yen Press, LLC.

Library of Congress Cataloging-in-Publication Data
Names: Uno, Bokuto, author. | Miyuki, Ruria, illustrator. | Keller-Nelson,
Alexander, translator.
Title: Reign of the seven spellblades / Bokuto Uno ; illustration by Ruria Miyuki;
translation by Alex Keller-Nelson and others.
Other titles: Nanatsu no maken ga shihai suru. English
Description: First Yen On edition. | New York, NY : Yen On, 2020–
Identifiers: LCCN 2020041085 | ISBN 9781975317195 (v. 1 ; trade paperback) |
ISBN 9781975317201 (v. 2 ; trade paperback) | ISBN 9781975317225
(v. 3 ; trade paperback) | ISBN 9781975317249 (v. 4 ; trade paperback) |
ISBN 9781975339692 (v. 5 ; trade paperback) | ISBN 9781975339715
(v. 6 ; trade paperback) | ISBN 9781975343446 (v. 7 ; trade paperback) |
ISBN 9781975352240 (v. 8 ; trade paperback) | ISBN 9781975369545
(v. 9 ; trade paperback) | ISBN 9781975369569 (v. 10 ; trade paperback)
Subjects: CYAC: Fantasy. | Magic—Fiction. | Schools—Fiction.
Classification: LCC PZ7.1.U56 Re 2020 | DDC [Fic]—dc23
LC record available at https://lccn.loc.gov/2020041085

ISBNs: 979-8-8554-0739-6 (paperback)
979-8-8554-0740-2 (ebook)

1 3 5 7 9 10 8 6 4 2

HJM

Printed in South Korea

Characters

Fourth-Years

The story's protagonist. Jack-of-all-trades, master of none. Swore revenge on the seven instructors who killed his mother.

Oliver Horn

A samurai girl from Azia. Believes that Oliver is her destined sword partner.

Nanao Hibiya

A girl from Farnland, a nation belonging to the Union. Has a soft spot for the civil rights of demi-humans.

Katie Aalto

A boy from a family of magical farmers. Honest and friendly. Has a knack for magical flora.

Guy Greenwood

A studious boy born to nonmagicals. Capable of switching between male and female bodies.

Pete Reston

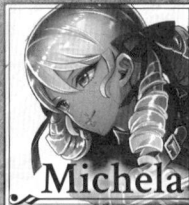
Eldest daughter of the prolific McFarlane family. A master of the pen and sword, she looks out for her friends.

Michela McFarlane

A lone wolf who taught himself the sword by ignoring the fundamentals. Determined to beat Oliver in a rematch.

Tullio Rossi

Michela's paternal half sister. Stubborn and headstrong, she has a competitive streak where Chela is concerned.

Stacy Cornwallis

Has served Stacy since they were kids and is dedicated to her. Half human, half werewolf.

Fay Willock

Heir to the Albright clan, known for its prolific warrior mages. His bulky frame radiates confidence and pride.

Joseph Albright

Fourth-Years

Cast a spell on Katie during their welcome parade. Has poor people skills and a sharp tongue that gets her in trouble.

Annie Mackley

A pure Koutz practitioner. Has been questioning her way of life ever since her match against Nanao.

Ursule Valois

A proud youth from a prestigious family. Recognizes Oliver's and Nanao's talents and considers them worthy rivals.

Richard Andrews

His every move is oddly showy, like a stage performer. Bedazzles with a blend of magic and deceit.

Rosé Mistral

Third-Years

Oliver's closest vassal. Adores him and aids his revenge as a covert operative.

Teresa Carste

Leoncio's younger sister. A fan of Oliver's since the combat league.

Felicia Echevalria

Teresa's friend. Has carried a torch for Guy since her arrival at Kimberly.

Rita Appleton

Seventh-Years

Student council president known and feared as the Toxic Gasser. Wears women's clothes as the whim strikes him.

Tim Linton

Katie's coresearcher. Lost the student council election, which has left her with debt.

Vera Miligan

Instructors

Kimberly's headmistress. Proudly stands at the apex of magical society.

Esmeralda

A new instructor at Kimberly and a famed mage. Like Pete, they're a reversi.

Rod Farquois

Magical engineering instructor. Prone to outrageous lessons designed to maim students.

Enrico Forghieri DECEASED

Chela's father and the man who sent Nanao to Kimberly.

Theodore McFarlane

Astronomy instructor. Driven to protect the world from tír incursions.

Demitrio Aristides DECEASED

A sword arts practitioner renowned as the Blade Master. Friends and rivals with Darius since their student days.

Luther Garland

Frances Gilchrist **Vanessa Aldiss** **Baldia Muwezicamili**
Dustin Hedges **Darius Grenville** DECEASED **Ted Williams**

Prologue

In a remote part of Lantshire lies a forbidden territory. Chasms where they claim even grass refuses to grow.

In fact, even mages avoid it to the best of their abilities. Should they be taken there, a dire fate almost certainly awaits them; venturing there of their own accord would mark them a fool of the highest order—or fatally off their rocker, no longer capable of distinguishing their home from the gallows.

"Hah...hah...hah..."

Staring up at the gray sky, gasping for breath, Godfrey hoped he was at least the former.

The training grounds within the Gnostic Hunter headquarters saw new recruits scattered across the property of this charnel house. Their welcome party had drawn to a close.

"Good enough. Done till 4D training. Until ordered otherwise, eat and rest."

With that, their instructor left. But those listening were in no state to do either of those things.

Corpses of magical beasts. Remains of golems. Piles so high, there was no safe place to step—and between them, craters large and small, gouged into the ground of the training area. The recruits lying there, out of breath, had nearly all sustained wounds far beyond a few broken bones, each in a state of extreme exhaustion—and fresh out of mana.

Ragged breaths were a good sign; some of them did not appear to be breathing to begin with. They'd rather have emergency treatment than food and sleep, but such practicalities were off the table here.

"...You alive, Lesedi?" Godfrey asked, managing to catch his breath.

"...Somehow. The two behind you?" his partner said, not getting up.

Godfrey staggered to his feet, moving to the two recruits nearby. They'd had it in for him at the start of training, but now—well, even being generous, they were half dead. Missing several limbs and long since unconscious, the recruits had wounds that would be fatal to any ordinary. But by Gnostic Hunter standards, the two of them were expected to heal up with a little food and rest.

Kneeling down to check their pulses, Godfrey sighed with relief. "Still breathing. Sorry, I'm not much of a healer—hang on till we reach the med ward."

"...Gimme one. I got enough left to carry."

Lesedi managed to right herself; even though she didn't have even a drop of mana left in her, she heaved one of the wounded on her back and set out. Godfrey followed, briefly considering collecting the severed limbs. But given the state of the training grounds, it would be nigh impossible to find them, and there was no guarantee they were intact. He quickly dropped the idea.

"And that was just a warm-up," Lesedi growled. "Can't even imagine how bad it is in the field. Especially if you plan to stick to *your* guns."

"......"

Godfrey merely nodded.

She eyed his profile a moment, then turned quietly to the front once more. "Another tour of hell. As if I hadn't seen enough of those."

A harsh truth, delivered without passion. That brought any number of memories to Godfrey's mind—the darkness on campus, the kind gestures of the best friend he'd lost, the lonely look of the junior he'd failed to save, the cheery bounce in the step of the comrade he'd left behind. What they'd been through was not something he could forget.

"I'm not about to let it stop at a *tour*," said Godfrey. "If I'm there, I wanna make it *better*. Like I did at Kimberly."

"Bold. You realize that's tantamount to improving the very world?" Lesedi replied, intentionally digging deeper, making sure he knew the implications—like she always did.

And that familiar back-and-forth put a confident smile on his face at last.

"Everyone says it's impossible," he told her. "In other words—it's just like the day we began."

His mind was made up. He'd do it all again. He'd moved from Kimberly to the world at large, his targets no longer students consumed by the spell, but Gnostics corrupted by tír gods. And yet, Purgatory himself remained the same.

Once more into the breach. Let them point their fingers, dismiss him as a fool. He was in the dirt, spilling his blood, all while praying that he'd be a mite better a fool than the last time.

CHAPTER 1

Separation

Early morning, the day after the fight in the lava tree mold beneath the irminsul. Guy had returned alive but cursed; he and the Sword Roses were visiting the workshop of the provisional curse instructor, Zelma Warburg.

"…Hmm…" Zelma grunted.

She had Guy standing upright and was prodding him all over.

Watching with bated breath, Katie couldn't stop herself from saying, "W-well, Instructor Zelma?"

"Anything to be done?" Oliver chimed in.

Finishing her exam, Zelma turned toward them.

"Long story short, not any time soon. The curse energy has acknowledged the host and attached itself. In that state, it might be infectious—but it won't *leave*. If I'm to forcibly remove it, I'll need a few months, minimum—and it could well take years."

"……!"

That dire proclamation made Guy wince and his friends turn pale. Zelma shook her head; this was not as bad as it sounded.

"Naturally, if needed, I'll do just that. But there's little point in rushing things. Baldia will stop by long before I finish the procedure—unlike Vanessa, the Gnostic Hunters've gotta be careful how they use her, so she's not exactly stuck on the front lines."

"…Oh?" said Katie.

"You mean—," Oliver began.

"She could yank this curse out in a second. She's your mother in curses, and there ain't a better host the world over. In other words, you'll likely only be stuck with it for a couple of months. That make you feel any better, Mr. Greenwood?"

Guy let out a huge sigh of relief. Oliver felt the same; Zelma was Baldia's substitute and clearly just as inclined to wind people up. She should very much have started with that information.

Katie was so relieved that she staggered, and Nanao caught her. Zelma watched with a twisted smile on her face before changing tacks.

"And there's a more positive take on that waiting period—you have a *choice* here. What kind of magecraft will you pursue? This gives you time to think on that."

"…Time to choose, huh?" said Guy.

"Yeah. And you know what I'm about talking about. That curse is thorny but could also be the gift of a lifetime. It's a fact that you came back alive from Lombardi's territory. The situation may have forced your hand—but that power is now your own."

Strong words, and Guy's gaze dropped to his hands. From the moment he'd taken on this curse, it had never felt *borrowed*. It had agreed with him far too well. Perhaps that was just proof of his aptitude for hosting it.

"Seems a waste to just let go of it. I'm not trying to back Baldia here, but I am a curse wrangler—and I say don't be hasty. Think it over. The next few weeks will make the pros and cons of curse wrangling all too clear. It ain't gonna hurt to make your decision in light of that experience, and I'll spare no effort to help you control it. Out of respect for your natural talents."

"B-but, Guy, a curse wrangler—?"

Katie's emotions spilled out—and Chela wrapped her arms around the curly-haired girl, a hand over her mouth.

"You must not say that, Katie," Chela urged, anguished. "It is not for us to decide what path Guy's magecraft follows. That is something each of us must fret over for ourselves alone."

"——!"

Katie took that admonishment to heart, hanging her head. No

matter how close they were, this was an unwritten mage law, and it could not be ignored. And one that came right back at her—more than anyone else here, Katie had proven insistent on following her own magecraft no matter how much anyone tried to stop her.

"Of course, it's not all sunshine and roses," said Zelma. "Living with curses means you gotta be careful in every aspect of life. The closer you are to someone, the easier it is to *transmit*. If you learn to control it, that's less of a concern—but practically speaking, you're gonna have to distance yourself a while."

Zelma was hammering that point home.

Weighing her words, Pete asked, "Then should we not share a workshop?"

"Better not, no. If you aren't a wrangler, safer to limit yourselves to conversation on campus," she told the group. "And to be very clear, don't go assuming we can just take it back off you if it does transfer. The moment it's hit you once, that's a *shared curse*. The longer that goes on, the more likely the 'host' goes from individual to your whole crew—and then you're *all* cursed."

A leaden silence settled over the room. Everyone was forced to see just what living with a curse meant, just how hard being a wrangler was. Like they could see their friend's shoulders diminishing in the distance. Without thinking about it, Oliver started to reach out his hand.

"...Guy—"

"Don't, Oliver."

That harsh voice made him freeze. As Oliver quivered, Guy took a step away, toward the curse instructor.

"Thanks for examining me, Instructor Zelma," Guy said. "I'll be heeding your advice and keeping my distance. Can I come to you with any problems?"

"Of course. Tonight, even. I'll leave half my bed unoccupied."

"Spare me those jokes. I got enough on my plate already." He sighed and turned from her. Seeing the sea of grave expressions, he scratched his head. "Can't exactly ask you not to worry," he told his friends. "But we gotta roll with it. I'm gonna let this stew a while. Maybe it's the opportunity I needed. I ain't exactly prone to introspection."

"N-no—"

Tears in her eyes, Katie took a step forward—and Nanao and Chela each put an arm around her.

"I know exactly how you feel, but you must control yourself, Katie."

"Indeed. Clinging to him now will only make this harder for Guy."

That made Katie stop, but her eyes were still pleading with him. Begging him not to go anywhere, her gaze filled with turbulent emotion. That resonated. Guy barely suppressed the instinct to reach out to her and was forced to tear his eyes away. He looked to the face of another friend.

"It's not like we'll be apart forever. Just a temporary separation," Pete said. "I'm not upset. Fix that curse and come on back."

"Ha-ha, appreciate it, Pete."

Guy very much meant that. If anyone else tried to pin him down, he wasn't certain he could hold out. So he ended this quick. He couldn't bear to look at Katie again, instead settling for waving over his shoulder at Nanao and Chela. Then he turned to the last of his friends.

"My bad, Oliver. Look after Katie for me."

"…You got it."

With no other choice, Oliver nodded. Guy stepped closer, standing almost shoulder to shoulder.

"Take it *all* on," he growled. "You can't afford to hold back here."

"___"

That took Oliver's breath away, but Guy was already past him and out the door.

Oliver was scared to even consider what that last phrase meant.

With Guy gone, the others left Zelma's workshop, wandering the halls in silence that was occasionally broken by Katie's sobs. Nanao did not once let go of her. Oliver stayed quietly close at hand. Ahead of them, Pete and Chela were whispering to each other.

"...He was taking it in stride."

"Yes...he likely saw this coming the moment he took the curse on."

Both of them had the same impression. Looking back, they were downright impressed by how little Guy had let himself waver. Yet, both knew he was struggling. Not just because Zelma had praised his wrangling skills—that alone, he'd merely have shaken off. Something else was making it hard for him to choose.

"...Ngh..."

To Oliver, the words Guy had spoken in that lava tree mold were key.

"...Fantastic," he'd said. "I can finally fight alongside you guys."

Even though Guy was harboring curse energy that would likely be taken from him in due time, he was *thrilled* to have it. There were three years of frustrations behind those words he'd spoken, and that scared Oliver more than anything.

"Avoiding infecting us is obviously important, but more than that, I feel Guy needs time to *think*," Chela said. "He's a mage at a turning point in his life—it's only natural. All we can do is give him space and watch over him."

She made her stance clear, and Katie nodded. The curly-haired girl said nothing but looked ready to burst into tears again.

Nanao hugged her tight. "Head high, Katie. I am by your side."

Pete turned back and joined the embrace. "You can't snivel forever! Throw yourself into classes, and two months will fly by."

"...Mm. Sorry, everybody."

Katie absorbed her friends' words of comfort and encouragement as she tried to recover her composure, but everyone knew that was no easy task. Guy had been her biggest pillar of support, and even a temporary loss would hurt—plus, there'd been signs this might not be temporary.

Oliver, at least, had to remain calm. Telling himself that, he took a deep breath...and saw a witch standing down the hall. A seventh-year student, hair over one eye—an old friend to the Sword Roses, waiting for them.

"You all look gloomy," she said. "I take it Zelma couldn't remove Guy's curse?"

"...Ms. Miligan..."

Katie gently extracted herself from the group hug, wiped her tears, and turned to face the Snake-Eyed Witch.

"I'm afraid not," Chela said, folding her arms in concern. "If Instructor Baldia returns, *she* can easily manage it, but before then—no such luck. And worse, Instructor Zelma is extremely impressed with Guy's aptitude for wrangling. Given that Instructor Baldia gave him the cursed seed..."

"I thought as much. Guy will have much to worry his head about. Still, no reason to fret about it. Every student with multiple talents goes through this once." Miligan hunched down, putting herself on Katie's eye level and smiling. "There *is* a solution to the curse itself, yes? Then watch over him, without undue concern. If I may be so bold, no matter what path he picks, it will not lead him away from his friends. Even I can be sure of that."

The Snake-Eyed Witch's gentle tone surprised not only Katie, but Oliver, too. He and Katie knew each other well, but this was exactly the sort of thing Miligan would *not* have understood when they first met. She'd had no clue why Marco had opened up to Katie and thought the only way she'd find an answer would be to open Katie's head and examine her brain. The truth had been all too obvious to Katie's friends, but this witch, deep into her magecraft, had been unable to make heads or tails of it.

Now, however, Miligan got it. She knew what Guy was going through, what choices he would never make—and she could use that to support her words of comfort. To Oliver, this was a marked change. Perhaps Katie had changed her. Once, Katie had sworn to paint this school her color, and three years of hard work may have paid off there.

"I'll add that you're not far from Guy's dilemma yourselves," said

Miligan. "You're fourth-years—it's high time you firmed up your majors. Katie and Pete seem to have a clear direction, but what of the rest of you? Research seminars will be recruiting soon. You can't keep dillydallying."

That warning pulled Oliver out of his reverie.

True, no matter how worried they were, they could not dwell on Guy. Seminar slots were limited, and the deadlines could be harsh. The slower you were to act, the less likely you were to end up where you wanted to be.

Everyone gave Miligan looks of respect and gratitude, and Chela spoke for them all.

"Right you are. The reminder is appreciated, Ms. Miligan."

The witch smiled back. Then Oliver remembered another concern and gingerly voiced it.

"...Um, is your debt...?"

"Cease asking me that each time we meet! I am steadily paying it off—think no more on it!"

She pursed her lips at him and stalked away. Oliver took that to mean he really need not worry. Perhaps soon, they would no longer see her hovering outside the school store with a look of longing on her face.

"Well?" Chela asked, swinging around. "Should we all make like Guy and give some thought to our futures? Perhaps consult with others from our year?"

"Yeah, good idea," Oliver agreed. "Katie, Pete, have you picked a specific seminar yet?"

He looked around. Katie sniffed and nodded, and Pete shrugged.

"I've got a few candidates in mind," he said. "Was planning on running them by you soon."

"Hrm, I have not spared it a single thought," Nanao grumbled, tilting her head and crossing her arms.

Katie slapped herself on the cheeks. "Yeah, I'd better get on that. If I get stuck on this, I'll just make things worse for Guy..."

Muttering to herself, she set out. Seeing how obviously unsteady she was, her friends immediately gave chase. She hadn't even mustered false cheer; there was little else they could do for her other than be by her side.

Meanwhile, after leaving his friends, Guy found himself in a position he'd gone his whole life without experiencing.

"...It's so quiet when you're alone. Though, I have got this curse kicking up a racket inside..."

He was muttering to himself on the way down the hall. It was the nature of curse energy to want to infect things—that could be strengthened or weakened, but it never went away. If the urge to do harm overwhelmed the wrangler's capacity, measures would have to be taken; although at the moment, that risk was small. It felt like a low, animalistic growl inside him, but the fact that he could keep it at that level spoke to his exceptional talent.

"...This ain't good. This is the price I pay for all that time spent looking after Katie? Can't get my brain to budge one bit when it's my own shit. And I ain't exactly got anyone I can talk to..."

It wasn't the curse that had him clutching his head. For better or worse, he went with his gut, preferring to throw himself into things, figure stuff out in conversation. Now he was forced into the exact opposite approach—no specific tasks to apply himself to, no one who could help him talk it out. He'd have to *think*, and that was not his strong suit.

As he racked his brain, he saw a familiar face coming his way. The moment their eyes met, he threw up a hand   without really thinking it through.

"Mm, yo, Mackley. Back up and running?"

"..."

She ignored this point-blank, sailing past. Guy turned around, calling after her.

"Hello? Can you hear me? Mackley?"

Still, she failed to respond. If anything, she sped up.

Guy put a hand to his chin, thinking.

"......Hey, Annie," he tried.

The ground practically detonated beneath her feet. Her white wand came out as she lunged, poking it hard against his throat, her voice a low growl.

"Call me that again, and you die."

"Gotcha. It was just a joke, so put the wand away. Before you catch this curse."

He put both hands up, and Mackley took a step back, still fuming. She waffled a moment, then withdrew her wand, folding her arms.

"What do you want?" she asked, like she was suddenly obligated to engage. "I assume you're not dumb enough to think we're friends now. Just because we went through some shit..."

"Hell yeah! I know we're friends. It'd be harder to act like strangers after all that. Or are you an old hand at those games?"

Before Mackley could retort, a new voice chimed in.

"Are we included in that?"

She and Guy both turned to find two others from their year—one male, one female.

Guy raised a hand, smiling. "What up, Barthés? Nice to see you both on your feet."

"Thankfully, yes. You really pulled us out of the fire this time. Allow me to formally thank you, Greenwood. Mackley, that includes you."

Lélia Barthé's voice was warm, but this provoked a frown from Mackley.

"Don't lump me in with his dumb ass. I didn't lift a finger for you. Barely bothered letting you tag along in case I needed a decoy."

"I think that moment came and went. Like the deer," Gui muttered.

"Oh, you wanna throw down? 'Cause I'm ready!" Mackley yelled, hand on her wand again, brow twitching.

"Relax," Lélia said, palms out. "Whatever your perception of it, we both feel like we owe you a lot. And failing to repay that debt will besmirch the name of our mistress, Lady Ursule. That much, I'm sure you understand. So if either of you are in trouble, just say the word. Lélia and Gui Barthé will do whatever is in our power to help."

Guy grinned at the pair of twins, who were clearly in much higher spirits than at any point in their labyrinth adventure. Not a connection he'd expected to make, but hardly one to snub.

"Ha-ha, thanks. I'm in trouble all the time, so good to know," he said.

He moved a hand as if to shake, realized he currently couldn't do that, and yanked it back. That alone seemed to be all Gui needed.

"Seems like you're in a bit of a pickle right now. Can't get that curse out any time soon?" Gui asked.

"...Basically. Which means I'm waiting for Instructor Baldia to pop in. And they're telling me if I'm up for being a wrangler, I shouldn't give it back at all."

"Ah, a curse instructor *would* say that." Lélia nodded. "Even without much expertise, I could tell that you pulled off quite a feat. There's any number of wranglers in our year, but safe to say you're head and shoulders above them."

At this point, more students passed by—and paused when they saw Guy.

"'Sup, Evil Tree?" said one.

"Congrats on surviving!" added another.

"...Uh?"

"How's it feel being a sixth-year's Final Visitor? Like turning over a new leaf?"

Guy just frowned, baffled by the mix of curiosity and respect—and worse, the name they'd called him.

"...Wait, I got lots of questions, but first—why're you calling me that shit?"

"It's your epithet."

"It happens sometimes. You become someone's Final Visitor, you inherent their name."

"Especially if you're studying the same field. Mr. Lombardi was all about curses transmitted through plants, and so are you. Why *wouldn't* you be the second-generation Evil Tree?"

"That ain't me at all! Who the hell started this?!"

"Who knows?"

"No clue, but it's everywhere."

Shrugging off his protests, the students moved on, leaving Guy sulking.

"...What a headache! Like they're conspiring against me!"

"Don't scowl. It sounds ominous, but it's mostly complimentary."

"Yeah. Even the older students respect you now. Don't read too deep—just own it."

The Barthés were putting a positive spin on it, which Guy wanted to protest, but practically speaking, he'd probably *have* to take their advice. He couldn't exactly go around grabbing everyone by their lapels and demanding they call him something else.

That interruption had stalled their chat, so Mackley turned on her heel.

"...We're done? Then I'm going," she said.

"W-wait, Mackley!" Lélia cried, grabbing her collar with a smile. When Mackley made a strangled noise, Lélia leaned in, whispering in her ear. "You know Guy's at his wit's end, right?"

"...So what?"

"You need it spelled out? Okay, let's try an analogy. You were about to get hit by a stampeding swordrhino. Someone jumped in front of you and got run over. They're in critical condition, and you're unharmed. What should you do?"

The sarcasm-laden metaphor made Mackley grind her teeth. She was big on not letting debts stand and couldn't exactly brush this off.

"I ain't injured, and I don't need nursing," Guy said with a laugh. "But this turn of events means I can't be around my usual crowd, and on my own—I guess the wheels in my brain ain't exactly spinning. I don't handle quiet well."

He felt he could turn to these three instead. Scratching his head, he laid out his predicament. They'd only just gotten to know one another, so the tenuous nature of their relationship was a comfort. Where the Sword Roses might easily catch the curse, this crowd was unlikely to. Picking up on that, Gui nodded, smiling. "So you need someone to bounce ideas off? No problem at all."

"Give it up, Mackley," said Lélia. "I've been wanting to have a proper chat with you anyway."

"Can't say the same! Leave me out of this! You're trying to weave a web around me till I can't rid myself of you!"

"Ha-ha-ha! Not entirely wrong, but it's more a hex than a web, really."

Her prey snared, Lélia started dragging Mackley away. A torrent of foul language spewed from Mackley's lips, but laughter drowned it out. As the volume rose, Guy thought, *Yeah, that's more like it*. He and Gui followed the girls.

"Mm? So Guy 'as to keep 'is distance? Alas, 'e will be missed," Rossi said, leaning his elbows over the back of a chair.

When the Sword Roses reached the lounge, they'd found Team Andrews already there and got to talking; they'd only just finished filling them in on Guy's situation.

"If you need merry made, turn to me," Rossi added. "My arms are long enough for everyone, yes?"

With a grin, Rossi spread his arms out, demonstrating. Naturally, all five students ignored his offer, looking past him.

"Andrews, Albright, you were a great help in the lava tree mold," said Oliver.

"Mm! A splendid performance!" Nanao agreed.

"We merely pitched in a bit at the end," said Andrews. "You got to the trunk faster than us, and Mr. Greenwood's safe return is primarily to his own credit."

"Proving his aptitude for wrangling at a critical juncture... Talk about cocky," Albright grumbled.

"Try 'arder, would you? It will take more than that to dissuade me!" Rossi was rocking his chair back and forth, kicking up a fuss. Deciding he'd been a bit too hostile, Oliver made a face and turned toward the Ytallian.

"...We're kidding, Rossi. Naturally, we're grateful to you, too. We were just deeply appalled by your tactless offer."

"Forgive us, Mr. Rossi," said Chela. "I feel exactly the same. I merely wanted to assert that even if there were a hundred of you, you all would not equal Guy's little toe."

"A pair of charming smiles, yet you 'url spiteful remarks! Do not make me start *liking* that!"

Rossi clutched his shoulders, shivering. Blocking that display from his peripheral, Albright got back to the point.

"Either way, you decided to follow Greenwood's lead and figure yourselves out? I'll lend an ear, but I can't offer much advice. My path is the Gnostic hunts—always has been."

"And I'm saying you needn't be that committed to it, Albright. In my eyes, you have a knack for teaching. A future where you've built on that foundation is entirely viable."

"Teach where? At what school? A house with no name is one thing, but I'm heir to the Albrights. I'd argue that's a path you should consider yourself. Sounds like you're fitting right in on the council."

Albright and Richard started arguing the point. Chela wiped a tear, touched that Richard would be so concerned about his friend's potential. Rossi, meanwhile, was just watching this play out with a smirk—when all eyes started gathering on him, he looked startled.

"Oh, me? I 'ave not spared a thought to it. My life is like a walk upon the clouds."

"...How like your fighting style." Chela sighed. "A classic example of someone who needs his feet on the ground."

"See, Nanao? We can't end up like him," said Katie.

"I am not a mirror to your own flaws! I 'ave good reason for my lack of plans—I swore I would defeat Oliver before I settled upon anything!"

"How many years are you planning on attending Kimberly, Rossi? That's a thorny path to follow."

"Ah! Ahh! Pete, your tongue 'as grown so 'arsh!"

Ignoring Rossi's passionate gasps, they turned their focus back to the raging debate. When he caught their looks, Richard broke off, clearing his throat.

"Pardon me. Fact is, those with multiple aptitudes always face a tough decision. Chela, Oliver, none more so than you. Meanwhile, those who have a single standout aptitude need merely pursue it to its fullest. Not to deliver the most stock advice possible, but it's true."

"Hmm, then in my case...," Nanao mused.

"Sword arts or brooms," said Chela. "Major in either, and Instructors Garland and Hedges will be waiting with open arms."

"It's very much worth attempting to attach yourself to one or the other. They both take picking apprentices seriously, but that makes it all the more worthwhile. And with you, Ms. Hibiya, it's absolutely in the cards," Richard assured her.

He wasn't quite meeting her eyes, but his bashful act failed to disguise the reverence behind his words. Oliver and Chela found that delightful and struggled to conceal it.

Albright nodded in agreement. "Aalto, Reston, the same approach should swiftly narrow your options. The opposite applies to you, McFarlane—but in your case, you're more likely to be bound by your house than your talent. Perhaps even more than I am."

"...I wouldn't compare us. But if I'm honest, I have my share of binds. I am not entirely at my father's command, yet..."

"...You'll have to tell us more about that someday. I know it's not easily shared...," Katie said, tugging at her sleeve. Chela immediately gave her an appreciative hug.

Albright shifted his focus away. "You're the one I'm most intrigued by, Oliver. Obviously, I'm well past dismissing you as a jack-of-all-trades. But acknowledging your abilities does not tell me where you're headed."

"___"

Oliver just stood there, lacking any immediate answer. Realistically, he could not imagine a future the way his friends could; he simply did not have that much time left. A fact he'd long since accepted—or so he thought, but now that turmoil came boiling back up. Trying to trample it down, he managed an awkward smile.

"Hate to disappoint, but honestly, I haven't even thought about it. Ever since I reached Kimberly, I've been too focused on the problems at hand. Never had a moment to look ahead."

"Aha! Much like myself!" Nanao crowed.

"Same—!"

"Hardly."

Rossi tried to jump in, and Pete cut him down.

A pleasant scene that cut Oliver to the quick. How sweet it would be if he had as much time as they did.

Albright closed his eyes, snorting. Oliver had expected a torrent of insults, but none seemed imminent.

"Hmph. Afraid I saw that coming," said Albright. "Take a moment to pull yourself out of other people's problems and deal with your own mess. Do not give me that same answer the next time we meet."

Some harsh words, but mostly sound advice. Oliver appreciated it, but today, everyone was being so nice, and that was just making it worse. Was the impact of Guy's withdrawal showing on his face? If so, he really had to get it together. He was in no position to go around revealing his weaknesses.

At this point, Richard took a step toward him. Interpreting Oliver's struggles to control himself as fretting about his future, Richard lent a helping hand.

"Consult with me whenever you like," he said. "If you want a lengthy chat somewhere out of the public eye, I know a good place in Galatea.

Should I see if I can wedge in a reservation for a private room this weekend?"

"Uh, thanks, Richard. I may…ask for that at some point, but not just yet. I want to give this a good think on my own first."

This generosity was too much for him, and Oliver threw up both hands, smiling. Realizing he was perhaps being overbearing, Richard backed off. Chela put a hand on Oliver's shoulder and smiled at him.

"It's not just Rick—many people here are eager to offer help. No need to rush things. The connections you've made are more valuable than anything."

Her warm words provoked a whole litany of emotions, but Oliver merely nodded.

With that topic settled, Albright looked at each face in turn.

"…One last word of advice," he said. "Not to any one of you, but the whole group—Greenwood included."

That sounded significant, so everyone straightened up.

"Don't get reckless," Albright growled. "Everything we've discussed is founded on the assumption that you will live to graduate without being consumed by the spell."

"……Yeah, point taken," Oliver managed.

Five heads nodded. The best advice they could receive—but to Oliver's ears, the irony of it was all too clear.

With that discussion over, they headed to the bulletin boards to see what specific options were available. When Katie saw the recruitment posters listing each research seminar's strengths, she groaned.

"So many choices… Even if I narrow it down to just magical creatures, there's still so much to consider."

"Not only the seminar's theme, but the faculty adviser, and the older students you'll be sharing a space with. Katie, why don't you simply follow Ms. Miligan's lead?" Chela asked.

"I've certainly considered it. But she's graduating this year… I'm taking over her research on demis on a personal basis anyway. I'd like to join somewhere that'll let me put that experience to good use."

"Hrm…a single glance at this makes my eyes spin," Nanao grumbled.

"Hiiiibiiiiyaaaa!" came an anguished voice behind her.

Everyone spun around to find their broom instructor grinning from ear to ear and managing to make that menacing.

"Oh, well met, Sir Dustin!" said Nanao.

"Yes, yes, that's me, all right! Hate to barge in on your peaceful comradery, but first, I must ask—if you're inspecting this board, you must be looking for a seminar, yes?"

"That is the general idea," Nanao replied, nodding.

Dustin clapped a hand to his face, his smile fading. He turned to look up at the rafters. "Why have you not come to me?! I've been waiting for you since the year began!"

"O-oh?"

"How many times did I tell you? 'In your fourth year, come check out the aerial battle seminar I run!' This makes no sense! Tell me you didn't forget? Do you even know how rare it is I actively recruit?!"

His voice shook. Reaching the obvious conclusion, Oliver and Chela each leaned in, whispering in Nanao's ears.

"…Go with him, Nanao. It's your choice whether to join, but you shouldn't spurn a teacher's invite."

"Yes, see the look on his face? He's beyond anger—those are tears in his eyes."

"Mm. Point taken!"

Finally recognizing the urgency of the matter, Nanao sprang into action, bobbing her head as Dustin escorted her away.

Pete snorted, watching her go. "Guess she's a lock on that one."

"I imagine she'll get a few serenades from the sword arts seminars, too… It's only a matter of time," Oliver said with a nod.

But as they watched their friend go, someone else came up from behind.

"Pardon me. Do you have a moment—especially you, Ms. Aalto?"

All turned around to find a sixth-year male wearing glasses. Oliver alone recognized him—not from school, but from the labyrinth. This was a comrade.

Faced with an unknown upperclassman, Katie, Chela, and Pete braced themselves. This was no overreaction, but a necessity of Kimberly life. The sixth-year smiled and put his hands up.

"No need for that," he said. "I am recruiting her, but today is no more than an introduction. That said, there are not many tír seminars, even at Kimberly."

"____!"

That word got Katie's attention. And her reaction encouraged him.

"I believe your interest and aptitudes would best be served with us. I'll brief the other members—feel free to stop by anytime you like. I'm sure you'll gain something from it."

With that short speech, he handed her a pamphlet and withdrew far easier than anyone anticipated.

Eyes on the paper in her hands, Katie said, "This *was* on my short list. Studying the gnosticized versions as an extension of demi biology and culture."

"And they came to you first? So you do have an interest in tírs, Katie?" Chela asked.

"...Yeah. Since that migration—but also, the more I study demis, the more I know I can't avoid the subject. Both with Gnostics and tírs, the magical world is sorely lacking in attempts to *understand*. It's not like I don't get the logic behind Instructor Demitrio's arguments against that, but..."

Katie had clearly been wrestling with that contradiction. Oliver peered at the pamphlet over her shoulder.

"I'm interested in that myself," he said after a brief hesitation. "Wanna scope it out together, Katie?"

"Huh? Oliver? Er, I mean, I'd appreciate the company..."

She had clearly not been anticipating this offer, and it rattled her. Pete and Chela exchanged glances—and that said everything.

"Nanao's already gone," Pete told the group. "Let's split up. I wanna check out a few candidates myself."

Katie looked surprised, but this was the right choice. No point in visiting a seminar far from your own field. Only those with a chance of joining had a right to visit—and that meant Pete would have to strike out on his own.

"Good idea," Chela said, backing him up. "I'll accompany Pete on his rounds."

"Yeah? Fine, but don't grumble if it bores you."

He hadn't expected that. Nonetheless, he shrugged and let her follow him.

Once Pete and Chela were gone, Oliver glanced at Katie.

"Shall we, Katie? He *just* extended the invitation, but I'm sure he won't mind an immediate visit."

"Um—sure…!"

She nodded and set off. Oliver joining her was nice and comforting—and also embarrassing. She was wrestling with the choice of seminars enough as it was without having a second source of consternation tagging along.

They reached the third-floor room listed on the pamphlet and found the upperclassman from earlier alone with his nose in a book. He was hardly the only seminar member—safe to assume this was not a prime gathering time.

"Oh, here already?" he said, breaking into a grin. "Lovely! Do sit down."

He got up and waved them to some chairs; they thanked him and took their seats. Meanwhile, he moved over the shelves on the wall and brought back a heap of binders.

"…These are…?" said Katie.

"Figured our research would be the best way to say hi. It's all on tír creature biology and communication attempts. Not a genre you'd find in the library, right?"

Katie blinked at him for a second, and then she dove right into the pile of documents. In no time, she was hyperfocused.

"You've got lots of data, then," Oliver noted—speaking not as a comrade, but as a fellow student. "I thought research like this was unofficially off-limits even at Kimberly."

"They act like it is for appearances, but I feel like it's actually the other way around. Otherwise, would they ever have given the go-ahead for Morgan's attempt? Our headmistress would never publicly endorse Gnostic research, but under the table, she's actively encouraging it. That's my impression, at least."

The upperclassman delivered this with an impish grin, filling Oliver's head with questions. If his comrade felt certain enough to make this claim, it was likely Kimberly's actual stance—but *the* Esmeralda, pro–tír research? That made no sense. Anyone as high up in the magical world as her would be pressured to match the Gnostic Hunters' opposition to it.

"That said, there are very few active projects going. Just obtaining a gnosticized sample or a tír creature means going through a hellish process. Still...Kimberly is definitely at the forefront of tír research. I think this place will get you closest to what you want to do, Ms. Aalto."

That gentle reminder made her pull away from the documents in front of her, and she snapped the file shut, straightening up.

"I'm sure you're aware, but last year, I made contact with a Uranischegar migration," she said. "I can't say I made proper observations—it was only for a moment."

"I know all about it. That experience led your decision to visit us?"

"...Basically. The connection we made—if that's the word for it— gave me a sense of the mind behind the migration. Or maybe it was more emotional? Its heart? The distance between us was vast, but I sensed common ground. Like we *aren't* fundamentally incompatible."

Katie's attempts to describe her experience made Oliver gulp. She'd said as much before, and he'd had no clue what to make of it.

"Fascinating," the upperclassman said, chin in hand. "You heard the voice of their god? And whatever the truth may be, that was your emotional response to it."

"...Yeah. Purely subjective, no real evidence I was right."

"That's fine. In the absence of other clues, mages proceed according to their instincts. So...what is it you want to *do*? In light of this unusual experience?"

Rather than debate the details of what she'd gone through, he prodded her intent. Katie's head went down; she picked her words carefully.

"At this point, I basically know nothing about Gnostics, tírs, or their gods. Yet, despite that ignorance, I'm told I must unilaterally treat them as my enemies. This feels wrong to me. Like I'm wearing clothes where the buttons are misaligned," she explained. "So my first step is to resolve that. No matter where it takes me, I have to begin by learning. I really haven't thought about what lies past that."

The upperclassman took all that in stride, arms folded. "So you're at that phase. Kind of a relief! If you'll forgive me for it, I was worried you were overeager and getting ahead of yourself. Common in students on the verge of being consumed by the spell," he said. "However, from what you've said, you're still in control. Demonstrating a desire to remain on this side of that line. This is a very risky field, so that desire can make all the difference. I'm not saying I'm without concerns—but looking out for those is what your senior fellows are for."

He spoke with a pleasant smile, and Oliver wasn't sure what to make of it. Was this simple benevolence? Lip service to a seminar candidate? Or a performance as a comrade? This man might serve Oliver, but that didn't mean Oliver could read his mind. Perhaps sensing that, the sixth-year turned to him.

"She's made herself clear. Mr. Horn, are your interests aligned?"

That made Oliver reset. He couldn't have Katie do all the talking. He was supposed to be interested in this subject—and that was, at least, partially true.

"More or less," he replied. "Most specifically, I'd like to research ways to reduce Gnostic incidents. Not by fighting and eliminating them but by tackling the root cause—preventing gnosticization in the first place."

He'd prepared that answer ahead of time, and Katie gave him an astonished look. He had not been able to bring this up in front of Richard, so this was the first she'd heard of his position.

"Then much of your work should overlap with Ms. Aalto's," the upperclassman said, smiling. "Neither are exactly typical Kimberly ideals. If you're that aligned, I see why you're together... Yes, you're a good match. I can tell you're on the same page deep down, and that should lead to good synergy in the future. I'd love to have you both join us—talking to you has only made me sure of it."

The upperclassman kept his tone pleasant but made his point clear. If they chose to join the seminar, they'd be welcomed—both took this as a promise. Now they merely needed to make up their own minds.

"I won't pressure you to make a decision now. I'm sure you have other places to check out. Stop by all you like over the next month or two and weigh your options. No need to limit yourself when you're not committed."

Both Katie and Oliver appreciated this lack of pressure. For a while, they read up on tír creatures, then thanked the upperclassman and left the seminar room.

In the hall afterward, neither spoke right away. How should she respond to what she saw? Katie wanted to sort it out internally first.

"...He seems nice," she said at last. "Other recruiters have been way more aggressive. This guy listened to what I had to say first."

"Yeah. Felt like his priority was figuring out where we were at. I think you made yourself clear."

This was his honest opinion, but Katie drew up short. Oliver paused, turning toward her—and she gave him a long look, then took a deep breath.

"If I chose that seminar…would you really join me?"

"Yeah. But if you don't, there's no chance of me going there solo. In that case, I'd rather come with you to inspect other places."

Oliver didn't hesitate to answer, and Katie had to stop herself from pouncing on it. She slowly put her next question on her tongue—the point she really couldn't let remain unclear.

"…Because I'm at risk? You're scared to let me be alone? Are you saying this to protect me?"

Her voice was intentionally forceful. Implying—though this was not the case—that she resented that implication. A pathetic performance, she thought. Given how much she'd relied on Oliver thus far, she really didn't want to act like this. But it had to be said. Depending on his motivation, this was a moment she might have to push him away no matter the consequences.

Oliver managed a forlorn smile. That alone took her breath away. She was struck with guilt that threatened to wring her heart.

"If I'm honest, that is part of it," Oliver said quietly. "But more than that, I want to work *with* you on the issues involving demis and Gnostics. You have perspectives and responses I lack. I've always admired that about you, and I'm looking forward to seeing what they produce. This isn't a new thing for me. I've thought as much since our very first year."

It came out so readily, it stung. He wasn't trying to put up a front—this was his heart's desire. She got that without having to ask again. There was no space for doubt. The bond between them was strong enough for her to know.

All words of rejection dissipated within her. In their place: a wave of sweet emotion rising from the soles of her feet, filling her body. *Uh-oh*, Katie thought. The edge of her vision spotted a place of refuge, and she leaped at it.

"...G-gonna hit the bathroom! Regroup at the lounge? Go on ahead!"

"Sure thing."

Oliver nodded with a smile, and she tore her eyes away, diving into the bathroom. She ran to the far stall and locked the door. No one could see her now. The moment she was sure of that, she put both hands on the door.

"......Ohhhhh......"

A wordless moan escaped her. And with it, a fountain of tears, dripping on the floor. Not out of grief—quite the opposite. From the tips of her toes to the tips of her fingers, bliss painted over every thought.

"...What is wrong with me...? Why does that make me so happy that I have to cry?" she rasped.

Of course it made her happy. Oliver had been the first person at Kimberly to empathize with her perspective. All this time, he'd looked after her, supported her, given her the push she needed—been her friend and her benefactor. Friendship and admiration and desire, every variety and shade, growing ever stronger. All had long since hit a threshold so high, there was no use even attempting to distinguish them. She felt every type of love for Oliver and had kept it all bottled up. To avoid taking him from a treasured friend. To avoid dragging him off to her spell.

"...Why am I like this? I know...he's already with Nanao. That was my last chance to push him away."

Her heart sank. She shouldn't have stopped to *verify*. She should have insisted she had to join the seminar alone, concocted some bullshit about a need for independence. She'd known that. But she'd been unable to breathe a word to that effect. Doing so would make Oliver distance himself. The boy who wanted to join her research would no longer be at her side.

And that wasn't an option. Not a choice she could make. She might have managed it before she knew his intentions—but not now that

he was in her hands. A sweet, warm *right* she could no longer let slip through her fingers.

"...Come back to us, Guy. You're...gonna break my heart otherwise..."

Katie sobbed again, calling their distanced friend's name. Joy and guilt in equal measure, churning within, no strings for her to grab, no hopes of unraveling the knot. Alone in a dark stall, she cried.

CHAPTER 2

Opportunity

Northern Lantshire. A chasm-filled wasteland, where the Gnostic Hunter headquarters stood—a charnel house feared the world over.

"*Merde.* Ah, I am fit to be tied. Vexed. Irate!"

One resident was striding down the hall. Fresh from the front lines, she bore the grime of battle—yet whether this witch counted as human was highly dubious. Her clothes clung to her captivating curves, but there were slits cut all over the cloth, and through those gaps peered *living eyes.* Compared with those, the barely dry blood covering the rest of her was but a fashion statement.

Yet, no one here reacted to these grotesqueries with fear. The warlocks in the hall gave way out of *awe.* Hierarchies here were downright primal; whoever had and would slaughter the most earned *reverence.* The means employed were merely in service of their duty.

"Vivere militare est."

This cypher made the iron doors part of their own accord. The witch stepped into a windowless room, and every gaze turned her direction. There were three individuals within. One was a towering figure nearly touching the ceiling, much of its bulk swaddled in pale cloth like a newborn babe. On this specter's face was a porcelain mask. The man beside it had replaced the lower half of his body with a spiderlike golem; above that, he appeared to be a gaunt, high-strung young man. And at the far end of the room stood a burly warlock in the prime of life, with all the gravitas of a monarch or a judge.

Few acts were more futile than wondering who these horrors might be. If, by some mistake, an ordinary beheld them, they would be but doom in different shapes. Told this was the entrance to hell that waited beyond their gallows, all would nod in agreement. Here was a place one step outside this realm—and the first sign of *humanity*, of recognizable displeasure, came from the man-spider. Folding the two extant human limbs, he followed his action with *words*.

"Hundred, even returning from the front, you can manage a better appearance. Why replace your makeup with grime? Did you split your prey above your head in lieu of a shower?"

"Hold your tongue, Arachne. I'm not in the mood. Can you believe it? I ran into Aldiss in the thick of it. Cleaning up her half-finished meals has left me with a towering rage—would you care to help me vent it?"

"Hrr-hrr-hrr-hrr...!"

A sinister noise emerged from behind the mask. This was accompanied by a gush of drool that quickly formed a puddle on the table. The resulting din resembled nothing more than the death rattle of aging pipes about to burst from the water pressure. The only indication that this was *laughter* was the way that towering figure shook, with violence approaching writhing. A laugh it was—just not that of anything *human*.

The woman called Hundred glanced once at the silent warlock in the back, then at her surroundings—then she raised a brow. She had not expected the jeers at her condition to end so soon.

"...Oh, is the geezer not yet here? Did he finally croak?"

An ancient voice crept up behind her. "Well, sorry to let you down."

She swung around to find a hooked-nose old man covered in rust-colored bandages, his back so bent, it was like his very skeleton had been crushed. The skin on his hands was so dry, it resembled bark. Yet, the eyes lurking in those hollow sockets were lit by a survivor's obsession powerful enough to override those prior impressions. He was as heinous as he was hideous, like a ghoul clinging to life by eating the guts out of babies.

"You led an assault on a Sacred Light base. How fared you, Hook Nose?"

At last, the warlock in the back broke his silence. A formal query, yet the ancient ghoul responded by spitting at his feet.

"An empty nest— Well, not entirely, but only rank and file left. Waste of my time. Not even a bishop there to amuse me."

The warlock's chin wobbled slightly; interpreting this not as a fidget but a nod, the eldritch witch and the ghoulish geezer took their seats. The spider needed no chair. The hefty table between them was held up by four bizarre legs—each a petrified human. No one here even noticed, let alone brought it up.

They were Gnostic Hunters. Those who protected the order of their world, slaughtering Gnostics, fending off contact with the tír. By any means necessary, by every means they could think up and acquire, abandoning morals, ethics, and humanity in exchange—and many of them did not even bother to retain human form. And the elite eliminators among them gradually slew their way to *leadership*.

Squint, and the proof presented itself. A looming pile of grisly corpses behind them, an aura no mage could possibly miss. This—and this alone—was unshakable evidence that they belonged *here*.

Collectively, they were known as the Ostrac Five Rods. Defenders of the world—and those who *defined* it. As threats bore in from tír lurking beyond the sky the masses beheld, the members' rods stood firm in that path, drawing a boundary between worlds. Like stakes driven upon the border, chains leaving no gaps between, closing off the very world. Looming like a vow to let *nothing* change. Firing back at anything that tried to step within. No matter who tried, they would kill it, burn it, and leave no ashes behind.

They killed so that the world would remain closed off, so that their order would remain everlasting. They trampled and incinerated any voice praying for salvation from beyond. No exceptions, no generosity, no compromises. The line they drew had never once shifted. Whether outside influence was invited or accidentally allowed in—there was no escape. All would succumb to their cleansing fires.

Naturally, they fundamentally did not employ namby-pamby bullshit like human rights. Acting like there was a baseline standard for dignity of life was equivalent to being picky about their methodology. And that would mean they'd fail to protect anything. If the need arose, they would light the very world on fire, and they firmly believed that the removal of that pretext would allow tír invasions. The resulting way of life was their spell, their magecraft—and in fact, by following it, they kept the world safe.

"Report in," the warlock said. "Walch, how fares the great sage you sent to Kimberly?"

The spider, Walch, chuckled. As arrogant as he was ghastly. Like he was providing a textbook example of how a mage ought to laugh.

"...They're stirring the pot, like I hoped," he said. "Not a word of protest has come our way—we can assume the situation has Esmeralda's hands tied."

"She lost three great mages in a row. If it was not her in charge, she'd not *be* in charge."

The ghoul cackled as if he was proof that living too long would distort one's laugh beyond recognition.

Between the two of them, Hundred scratched her head.

"...That bitch's face has got me pissed off again. Old man Denis, have you any Sundew's Blight leaves? Those really clear my mind."

"Uh...yeah, I got 'em. But they're brainrot poison, y'know. Louisa, you are the one witch alive who smokes 'em like cigarettes."

"Then fork one over. Or I'll walk right out this door and have my way with the first man I see. I'm fine with that, but before I report in? Well, that'd be *your* problem."

She shook her head as she spoke, and flecks of dried blood in her hair scattered on the table. Walch's brow furrowed, and his lips pursed.

Plunged indefinitely into frontline fray, Hundred Louisa had long since lost any hygienic impulse; no matter how filthy she looked or how badly she stank of rot, she still had a siren's charm capable of drowning any man. And she'd honed her self-control to the point of ignoring any unpleasant side effects. Thus, she could not even be bothered to chant a single purification spell.

The ghoul, Denis, sighed, then reached for his pocket, retrieving a long, thin leaf. Louisa snatched it away, pulled a white wand from her hip, and lit the leaf with a wave. Light crimson smoke rose, and she puckered her lips, inhaling it into her lungs.

"Haaah—"

A blissful exhalation. No papers or pipes required—her skill at spatial magic made this effortless. That McFarlane dandy had once said it lacked flair, but the wave of clarity drove that memory from her mind. Louisa was a firm believer in silencing her brain's attempts to dwell on the trivial.

"...I'm sure...there won't be a fourth. It's an internal feud, clearly," Louisa whispered, crimson smoke curling from her lips.

Walch nodded, fussily brushing the blood flecks off the table. "That's the most realistic explanation. Grenville, Forghieri, Aristides—if the three of them went down in rapid succession, some smoldering fire in the faculty ranks has likely burst into an inferno. With that lineup, they're not short on reasons. Still..."

He clicked his tongue. Even this spider was disinclined to sneer at the magnitude of this loss. Each mage he'd mentioned had no substitute on the front lines and, even in the back, had been indispensable in replenishing their forces. He had no intention of diminishing that work.

Thus, the full force of his scorn was devoted to the unacceptable failure of the witch who'd been in a position to prevent their loss—yet had not.

Aware of his feelings, Denis said, "Too soon to say if three deaths will be the end of it. But either way, well worth sending Farquois in there now. If there's a fire burning, they'll dampen it; if not, it still suggests their arrival is what put an end to the matter."

"Precisely. And it gives the impression Esmeralda could not resolve things on her own. Even if it actually was already over."

Walch's lips curled in a sneer.

Louisa had been listening absently, her eyes unfocused, but now she said, "What I followed of that was amusing. Basically...she's in deep shit? That's nice. That's very nice."

She smiled, as if that was all she needed to hear. No effort to disguise her malice, her attitude going beyond honest into downright innocence. Like a child laughing because someone they hated had messed up. Far past attempting to curtail such impulses.

Inhaling a third puff of smoke in a nigh death euphoria, Louisa thought, *When did I get this simplistic? When I was unlucky enough to survive getting part of my brain blown out in battle? Or when my house's deepest desire turned my body into a show window for enchanted eyes? I'm no longer sure. It doesn't matter. Perhaps I'm a bit stupider. But life is so much easier now.*

"It's going well, then," the warlock said. "But this gives Farquois unnecessary status and credit. I have no intention of underestimating their charm—keep a tight collar on them."

Walch folded his arms, looking sour. "Esmeralda would merely silence a lesser pawn. With that in mind, we have to turn a blind eye to their antics—to a degree. I'm sure you're well aware they've long had a disturbing enthusiasm for Kimberly's labyrinth. Once Esmeralda is pried from the headmistress's seat, we'll allow them to study those depths—that's the deal I struck," he explained. "Even I have to admit they're a mage worthy of the great sage moniker. Yet, that also means I recognize they care more about their own research than anything else and will not lightly relinquish the right to progress it. Especially if doing so would risk us turning on them."

Walch was firm on this point. And he had one more.

"But there are always exceptions. If they use this position to attempt to take control of Kimberly, then I'll go there myself to take them down. Or I'm not Alphonse 'Arachne' Walch. Or is that still not enough for you, 'Judge' Albright?"

Arachne put his pride on the line, but the warlock to end all warlocks, head of the Five Rods, Victor Albright did not even flinch.

"Being as cautious as you are is a virtue," Denis said, his cloudy eyes turning toward their leader. "But high time you agreed, Victor. Even if Farquois goes a bit too far, they're not gonna get the better of Gilchrist."

Denis was backing Walch from his own perspective. The Supreme Witch of a Thousand Years—the mere mention of her name made the room grow tense. A fact that Denis seemed to find amusing.

"Allow me to repeat myself, though I'm sure you're all sick of hearing it. Eight times. Eight! I have gone up against her and been cut to ribbons. Laugh away! It's now a show we put on once a century. It is what it is. She's a monster, pays no heed to me, to those swarms of reapers, to the very passage of time— Ha! And you think she'll be foiled by a youth not yet three hundred? Don't make me laugh. The richest of all delusions."

Denis slapped his knee. A joke at his own expense but backed by a vehemence even the Five Rods head could not ignore. Even in her drug-addled state, Louisa did not dare speak. She felt on her skin that doing so would mean her head leaving her shoulders.

A long silence lingered. The sort of calcified silence that took tremendous willpower to break. Once he deemed enough time had passed, Walch did just that.

"We'll all admit: Esmeralda's lead was an effective choice to quell the tumult that followed the loss of Two-Blade. But her task has come and gone. She cannot prevent rifts between the faculty beneath her—proof her powers are waning. We should drag her down now. While she's still capable of returning to the field as a Gnostic Hunter."

A weighty declaration. He, too, was highly focused, attempting to persuade Victor. His true motives revealed themselves beneath that thick layer of contempt, which Denis took as a sign he was too young. Yet, he was disinclined to criticize or jeer, aware the other Five Rods were not a thousand-year-old vintage like himself. Walch had yet to swallow anything like the filth Denis had choked down. Meaning that there was still a trace of virtue buried deep in those inflamed guts.

"......——"

Watching the leaf burn itself out, Louisa closed her eyes and opened them again. That alone cleared her stupor, and she was once again a Gnostic Hunter.

Better to be arrogant, then. As haughty as she could be. That was the baseline requirement for the four of them to match Judge's rigidness. Only when they balanced him out did the Five Rods begin to function.

"...It's the spice they need. That woman won't lie down and let the sage take over. Let them pull each other's sleeves. Not like I have any love for either."

"Hrr-hrr-hrr-hrr...!"

The specter quivered again. With this creature alone, that was all the indication of intent they required. More than any words could accomplish, this demonstrated that *they* were the ones who should be feared. Judge would not bend on that point—and so he nodded. This place bore the Five Rods' name; therefore, he was obligated to show the arrogance befitting the head of the Gnostic Hunters. Much as he had demanded—and still demanded—of his young son.

"Very well," Judge said. "I'll acknowledge I have no specific concerns about the great sage at present. On to the next topic: the great conjunction with Uranischegar next year. How will the Sacred Light move to prepare? Speak your views."

The mood shifted to something more productive. Tapping a finger to the side of his hooked nose, Denis went first.

"A Pentagon—Evit -was spotted in McFarlane's territory. One of a number of suspicious actions all over the place. But it doesn't feel like next year's their main goal. They're forever showing glimpses to keep us on our toes. We lack anything definitive to suggest a large attack."

"The augers aren't giving us much," Louisa said. "I'd say next year's unlikely myself. Lacking the pieces for a proper summon?"

"Mostly in agreement…but the rate of gates opening will go up. Like any standard year, there's bound to be at least one major incursion. I'd like our intelligence division to dig a little deeper, ensuring they don't hit us from behind during that. Naturally, I'm aware of how risky it is to send spies into a Gnostic group."

Walch wasn't missing the chance to press this argument. The inadequacies of their intelligence division had been a long-standing issue for the Gnostic Hunters; they were an extremist group, and that lent itself poorly to the delicate communication required to infiltrate. Since Victor took over, they'd at last founded a specialist division and begun training the rare candidate with any aptitude for it. To protect a world without changing it, they'd have to change themselves—a contradiction staring them in the face.

After three hours of furious debate, the topic wound down. Fresh from the field, Louisa was looking exhausted.

Denis made a show of rubbing his back. "These long sessions take their toll on these old bones," he muttered, but the ravings of a warlock were not worth listening to.

Point-blank ignoring him, Louisa leaned back in her chair, eyes on the ceiling. Every enchanted eye on her followed that gaze.

"I'd say that's enough. Too much formal talk! Let's throw in something light before we split. Walch, how fares the new blood?"

The spider looked annoyed but answered readily enough.

"I scoped out the training, and they're coming along well. A few caught my eye."

"What about them?" she asked, prodding a hazy memory. "The two with the biggest attitudes at the start? They were Kimberly kids, right?"

Denis chuckled. Those they talked about were unaware they'd already been marked as nails worth hammering down.

*   *   *

Students getting consumed by the spell might be an annual occurrence at Kimberly, but the lava tree mold incident had certainly sent ripples through the campus. The discovery of new territory in the labyrinth alone was the topic of much debate—but more than anything, the way the incident had ended had been unthinkable in any normal year.

"I doubt anyone here has forgotten the Kimberly faculty regulations," Headmistress Esmeralda begin, her icy tones echoing through the emergency faculty assembly.

The faces listening were even tenser than usual. Given the reason for this meeting, none believed it would end well.

"When pupils are lost in the labyrinth, we leave rescue operations to the students. Faculty directly take action only when eight days have passed after they are lost. No matter what relationship may exist between the students in need of rescue and the faculty. Even if they are your personal apprentices."

All knew this rule. A famous principle of Kimberly, part of their *Your life and death are in your own hands* philosophy. The instructors would not keep students safe.

"We do allow a modest amount of flexibility based on the specifics of the incident. In this particular case, the choice was made to urge evacuation when things first went wrong. And in the latter half, we stepped in to handle the curse on the irminsul, preventing the corruption of the entire second layer. I have no intention of rebuking Williams, Hedges, or Warburg for doing so. I have my concerns about them reporting these actions after the fact, but I will accept the excuse that time was a factor."

Each instructor she'd named quivered. They were glad to get away with it, but a clear line was drawn. They could go *this* far. But what about beyond?

"And yet, as the students attempted a rescue in the hollow beneath the second layer, someone made unauthorized, independent contact with them and proceeded to escort them to safety. This is a very different matter. This is a violation of the faculty code of ethics, with no wiggle room allowed—a clear mockery of the Kimberly way. Even if the individual responsible is but a temporary substitute."

All eyes turned to the far end of the table—to the mage on the receiving end of these remarks. Everyone present knew. There had only ever been one person this meeting was about.

"That is my perception of things. Speak your piece, Farquois. While you still have a mouth to speak with."

Esmeralda prompted the great sage to respond. Tensions mounted, but the mage themself appeared entirely unconcerned.

"'My piece,' is it?" Farquois snorted, shrugging. "I suppose I could babble a thing or two, but I just don't get it. I mean, what am I making excuses for? Students were in trouble, and a teacher went to their rescue. The most natural thing in the world."

Here at their official rebuke, they chose to directly oppose the core of Kimberly values. Several teachers looked resigned already, convinced this was tantamount to suicide.

"No defense, and no remorse. I am to take your position as such?" Esmeralda asked.

"Basically. But I do have an argument. Do you mind if I speak to that, Headmistress?"

"I will hear it. But consider your words carefully. They may be your last."

She folded her hands on the table.

"Then let me begin!" Farquois cried, as if given a chance to make a speech. "This school is an absolute disgrace. Gathering the finest unpolished gems from around the world, throwing them into the crucible, uselessly killing one another, and those lucky enough or plucky enough to survive get trotted around as if they prove you are a school of any excellence. The nerve of you. An issue far before the quality of your instruction. This environment does not even qualify as an institute of learning."

"Stop this, Farquois!" Dustin roared, unable to listen further.

The headmistress shot him an icy look. "Sit down, Hedges. I told them to speak. You have no right to silence them."

Dustin ground his teeth—but if he did not obey, he would lose everything below the knees. Forced to take a seat, he could only glare at Farquois, although that desperate warning went unheeded.

"Why did I act to save those students? For the simple reason that I did not wish to lose any of them. Every student who entered here is an unpolished gem with talent of infinite value. Each and every one of them has the potential to achieve incredible success. Our first responsibility as teachers should be protecting their futures—not kicking them in the back off the edge of a bottomless cliff. You may be satisfied only with the students who crawl their way back up, but those who perish without managing it should have had a path as well. So this time, I went down after them. And what possible problem is there with—?"

"Gladio."

A spell cut off their speech—and the sound of something falling echoed through the room. The teachers gulped, and Farquois glanced down.

The great sage found their own arm severed at the shoulder.

A beat later, a spurt of blood dampened the floor. Dustin's and Ted's chairs fell over.

"Headmistress! You can't!"

"They've been sent by the Gnostic Hunter headquarters! You know what killing them means!"

Both moved in front of Farquois, an action that could well spell their own deaths. But it had to be said, even if it cost them their own limbs. The cost of souring relations with the Gnostic Hunters would be far greater. At the same time, Ted was greatly relieved the librarian, Isko, had not been invited. At the least, *she* would not lose her head.

Observing this desperate act from behind, Farquois winced, then raised their remaining arm. The blood from the shoulder wound had already stopped—and not a trace of any pain appeared on their face.

"Calm down, gentlemen. If she was trying to kill me, she'd have aimed for the head. I could tell, which is why I took no action. Still— ha-ha, most impressive. I did not even feel the cut."

"This is a countdown. Consider yourself fortunate you have three chances left. Use them well." Esmeralda put her athame away and folded her hands once more.

In other words, she intended to go limb by limb, then finally take their head. This was the price she'd take for them insulting Kimberly to her face. Arguably a sign of her generosity.

But down this path lay nothing good. Convinced of that, Ted clenched his fists, summoning his last ounce of fortitude—and forced his voice from his throat.

"...I-if I may have permission to speak, Headmistress?"

"What, Williams?"

Her gaze drifted sideways, as if considering adding another limb to the mounting pile. Ted's survival instincts reflexively tried to seal his lips, but he powered through.

"...Th-this incident is partially...our failure to grasp and maintain the full scope of the labyrinth. This...played a role in the predicament the students faced. G-given the three missing instructors, we *could* assess the labyrinth's danger level as significantly higher than average. Since the students were stranded in uncharted territory, I have...some doubts as to whether leaving this incident in student hands was..."

Listening to his faltering attempt, Dustin swallowed. A very basic argument, nothing that would catch anyone by surprise. But voicing it here took such strength of will. He had infinite respect for the way their weakest instructor stuck to his guns.

In response, Esmeralda narrowed her eyes. "So you wish to argue that faculty failings played a role in the cause of this incident, meaning we should not force the resolution entirely on the student body."

"…I feel we were not on our best game. That is why I chose to take action myself. Arguably, Farquois's choices are an extension of what we did. I—I admit, they went out-of-bounds. But at the moment of intervention, it was impossible for anyone in the lava tree mold to know what was about to happen. The fourth-years were exhausted after their battle with the consumed sixth-year; there were valid reasons for staff and faculty to offer support."

Ted was clutching at straws. The missing teachers proved something was wrong at Kimberly, and the faculty had to adapt in response. In no way did that go against the school style—Ted himself was a graduate and was well aware of the value of this environment. But that did not mean he was willing to sacrifice students. Even if their lives were but fodder for the fires, they should be prepared, and the time should be ripe. He did not wish to rob students of that.

As Ted's speech dried up, the room fell silent. In that hush, his hand wandered unbidden to his throat. He would not have been the least bit surprised to find it already severed.

Meanwhile, Dustin was glaring at Farquois with nigh murderous intent.

Hold your damn tongue. My friend is sticking his neck out for you, and if you trample on that effort, I'll kill you before she can.

His eyes made that message loud and clear. With a ferocity that gave even the great sage pause.

"Mm, let's take a deep breath, Emmy," said a voice.

Dulcet tones from the ceiling. A figure came in to land behind the headmistress. A smiling man, his hair in ringlets, clad in a dark brown suit. His entrance was now routine; it provoked no surprise. The right hand of the Kimberly witch—part-time lecturer Theodore McFarlane.

"…Theodore."

"You've noticed, yes? He's trying to protect you more than he is the great sage. Even if that is not all that motivates him."

Theodore smiled at Ted, and the great sage turned their attention to the new arrival.

"It's been far too long, McFarlane. Popping up at this juncture? How laissez-faire."

"I came as soon as I could. Honestly, you're the last person I expected to be posted here. The Five Rods really do have a mean streak... **Flamma.**"

A sigh on his tones, Theodore cast a spell, and the flames arced from his wand to Farquois's severed arm. The great sage watched it crumple to ash.

"The arm you have left is apt penalty for your violation," Theodore said, unusually grim. "You must know how generous that is. I trust you have no complaints, Mx. Farquois?"

"Oh, I don't mind at all. An arm is a small price to pay for the salvation of my precious students. I'll just grow three extra for next time."

Farquois shrugged it off in good humor.

"I would not recommend joking," Theodore said, shaking his head. "Assume I cannot hold her back forever. Great Sage, it is high time you understood the nature of the witch you face."

Farquois's eyes narrowed. They understood this was not a threat, but a warning. Farquois looked back at the headmistress, and her gaze locked on them, never once wavering.

She showed no fear. Not of Farquois himself, nor the Gnostic Hunters' scheme behind them. Her eyes were a testament to the fact that she was prepared to take down the Five Rods if she had to. That she had no intent of playing around in their political farce. That was what the pinnacle of the magic world meant.

"...There will be no countdown next time, Farquois."

"...Haah. Point taken."

As they acquiesced, the doors blew open. A prompt to vacate the room—and with their wounds, the great sage was disinclined to refuse. Every eye followed them out, the doors closed behind them.

Farquois sighed. "My word! When was the last time I felt a chill run down my spine?" they muttered.

And they set off, smiling warmly at the students gasping at their missing limb. It was all *enjoyable*: the pain from the severed arm, the cold sweat on their back. It had been so long since this mage felt either sensation.

The morning meeting had narrowly avoided fatalities, but that was just the start of Kimberly's day. Once more, Guy was avoiding the Sword Roses, and that weighed upon him; as lunch began, he made his way toward a practice room.

"...Hmph..."

Moments after announcing his arrival, the room's master appeared and led Guy to a different classroom without so much as a word. David Holzwirt waved his student to a chair, then sat down across the table from him, arms folded.

"I swear I didn't plan to end up like this," Guy said ruefully. "Gonna be stuck with it at least two months—dunno what to do with myself. Being this cursed, I can't exactly play around in the dirt—and I sure can't take that tour of your research space."

He was light on explanations. Any mage could tell how much curse energy he harbored.

David merely nodded. "...I'm aware of your condition, including the unavoidable cause. I've got no plans to chastise you—but practically speaking, I can't let someone in your condition into the conservatory. There's a high risk you'll not only destroy the growing plants but also the entire biome. I'm sure you know that."

"Well aware. I figured I was banned till this curse is handled. Given all the plants I was handling, I'm dumping a lot on you."

"Maintaining the status quo for a couple of months is no big deal. I won't need to lift a finger—older students who think you've got potential will step in of their own accord. You might owe them a favor or two, but nothing to worry about there," said David. "What I want to probe is your intent. Can you truly promise this will end in two months?"

He fixed his student with a piercing gaze, and it took Guy's words away. He'd seen this question coming and delayed this visit because of it. Yet, even now, he did not have a clear answer.

"...Honestly, I'm still waffling. Instructor Baldia's been trying to pull me to her field for a while. Instructor Zelma's doing the same. Saying the fact that I've accommodated this curse proves I've got the knack."

"...I'd imagine. Even I can't argue with your aptitude. Especially after seeing several similar cases in the past. Including one you know too well."

"...Lombardi?" Guy said, taking the hint. The older student he'd faced, fought, and slain with his own hands.

"He was a promising student," David said, sighing and letting himself dig into his memories. "Treated the flora with tender care, never became impatient even if they did not grow the way he'd wanted. I saw him sit three days and nights by the side of a planter once. Never imagined he'd be consumed before graduation. Or that he'd rush for results like that..."

Guy had never had any real interaction with the man before the spell consumed him, but these few lines painted a vivid picture of the boy Lombardi had once been. Patient, placid, knowledgeable—he'd likely been an excellent mentor, too. Even after he'd been consumed by the spell, he'd shown signs of those traits.

"I'm not saying becoming a wrangler changed his nature. I'm sure he had his reasons for his haste," David added quietly. "He may not have been successful, but his research into employing the irminsul for curse processing is hardly meaningless. From the data he left, we've determined that the construct itself is viable up to a certain threshold.

There's a chance that'll be employed somewhere else to better effect someday. Not sure that'll help him rest easy, but…"

Guy nodded along with that. As they handled the cleanup in the second layer and the lava tree mold, David had collected his old student's papers. Perhaps he'd left a letter to his former mentor—Guy was convinced he had. Mage mentorships were not so fleeting as to be broken just because they'd gone their separate ways.

"Can't pretend I don't have a few choice words for Baldia—and having it all go down a second time is hardly pleasant."

David's eyes turned back to Guy, who straightened up. He got that. David was speaking not of the past, but of his own present.

"You saw how Lombardi died; I need say little else. Think carefully. Consider what you stand to gain and lose. Don't just imagine what you'll end up with—be dead certain of it. I'm sure he did the same."

"Got it."

Guy nodded, fully accepting this. He still had no ideas in mind, but these words would stick with him.

After leaving David, Guy wandered the halls, dragging his feet. He'd consulted a mentor—but that had not opened any concrete paths.

Guy felt that David had pointedly stopped himself from doing so. Words from a teacher had influence; he could have easily talked an inexperienced fourth-year into sticking with his field. If he'd just said it'd be best for him, Guy could not have dismissed that. But that was not what David wanted. Even after Lombardi's demise, he preferred to let his students choose their own paths. Despite knowing that the results could well repeat themselves.

Guy truly had found himself an excellent teacher. He would love to keep learning under him—that impulse was rising within. He was well aware that was the natural choice. Not turning against his character, not worrying his friends.

"…Ngh…"

And yet—that meant abandoning the strength he'd obtained. Retreating from the line he'd finally reached, from being able to fight alongside his friends. He knew no one would hold that against him. He knew they wanted nothing more than Guy Greenwood as he had always been.

But he also knew that if he stopped himself, his friends would go on ahead.

Each would follow their spell. Choose their ends. Head out to depths he could not reach.

While he was left behind, in the light—

"Hello."

A voice pulled him out of his thoughts. He looked around and found a younger girl—a third-year student, Rita Appleton. A diligent, hardworking, somewhat reticent girl, they'd met during her orientation and grown fairly close. If Katie was a handful of a little sister, this girl was one who didn't need his help and thus worried him just as much.

But after what happened in the lava tree mold, meeting her took on a different meaning. He did his best not to let that show, trying to act like his old self.

"'Sup, Rita. You here to chat with the teach? I just paid him a visit."

"I've been waiting for you. I knew you'd come by."

She almost talked over him. Regardless of whatever baggage Guy had, she was clearly not her usual self.

Rita seemed to have made her choice. She stood before him with a clear desire to share that choice with him.

"I heard from Instructor Zelma. You'll be away from your group for a while, until the curse is handled."

"Uh—yeah, basically. If I'm around them, they'll…have to watch themselves."

He went along with this, somewhat flustered. Rita was not normally the one to lead a conversation, which made it that much harder for him to act as he usually did. The thoughts he was dragging from his conversation with David made that worse. His nerves made his tongue falter, but he forced it to waggle.

"Well, you know. Shit happens. It's messing me up, though—can't even touch my friends."

And the result—what he *really* thought slipped out. Rita smiled, stepped forward, reached out both her hands—and took Guy's. Despite his condition.

"Huh?"

"Go ahead."

She pulled his hand to her chest. He felt the soft mounds, her warmth, her heartbeat—and his brain locked up, awash in sensation. He couldn't think straight. Unable to process the feedback from his senses, he couldn't move a finger.

"You— Why? Huh? What?"

"You long for human warmth, yes? Take your fill. Though, I'm sure this is no substitute."

"L-let go!"

His mind finally caught up. He tore his arm away from her, and she released him, his fingers adrift in space. He quickly looked inside, feeling out the curse energy. Relieved to find it had not transmitted, he sighed and, without recovering at all, fixed her with a glare.

"What are you even thinking? You know what state I'm in! One glance at me, and you know how contagious I am! Every part of my life's gotta change, even how I treat people! I can't get you mixed up in this!"

"I know. But I *want* to be part of that change. There was never an opening for me to wedge myself into. But now there is."

If he'd yelled at Rita like this any other day, she'd have teared up—but today, she took it with a smile. That stunned him, and she let a trace of guilt show.

"I'm sorry for phrasing it like that," Rita told him. "Just to be clear, I don't want you to become a curse wrangler. I love how you smile as you dig; I love how you always smell like sunshine. I just want to share that light with you."

Affection she'd long held close to her chest. Putting it out there, Rita reached for the buttons on her shirt. The breast he'd just palmed and the undergarment containing it came into view, and Guy flinched, turning away.

"......! What the—?! Put your clothes back on!"

"Don't worry, I'm not getting ahead of myself. I don't have the kind of figure suited for that approach. But I want to show you something—unsightly as it is."

Her voice sounded eerily calm, and that baffled him enough to risk a look—and his eyes caught sight of what lay between the sides of her opened shirt. At what she really wanted him to see.

"...You're, uh..."

"Yes. I'm got one, too. Some*thing* nesting inside me."

Her voice held a hint of self-derision, and Rita began doing up her buttons again. This revelation left Guy's brain boiling over, but she just kept talking.

"This is why I've been visiting Instructor David regularly. Honestly, I can't say it's fully under my control. Regular inspections were a condition of my admittance. The magical world is very harsh on these things. I'm sure you're aware."

Guy very much was. Given Katie's recent direction, he was no longer in a position to remain indifferent. But not in a million years had he imagined he'd see something like this close at hand. Especially roosting in a friend's body.

"Would you like to research it?"

"Huh?"

Rita's offer made his eyes go wide. She didn't give him time to recover. Her head was down, a rueful smile on her lips.

"Not a sample you can find anywhere else. It's inside me, under a degree of control—far easier to handle than anything in the world.

And that would work for me as well. There's a limit to what I can investigate on my own person. I can't even properly anesthetize myself for observations," she told Guy. "So I've been searching. Ever since I got here, I've been looking for someone I could trust with my body."

With that, Rita lifted her head. The look in her eyes spoke to the strength of her desire—and Guy could not move a muscle. This was not a topic he could take on anytime soon. Yet, he felt she would crumble to dust if he fled from the decision. Such was the desperation behind her act—Guy could not afford a careless move.

"With you, I'd give you everything. If you'll take it, my heart, too. As pushy as that may sound."

She offered a fragile smile. Words far too forlorn for a reveal of a love long hidden—Guy clutched his brow, hanging his head, squeezing words out from his confusion.

"Why...why are you saying this now?"

"Now is my only shot. I'm sure I'll never get another chance to steal you from Ms. Aalto, to pry you from the Sword Roses. You know I'm right. You love them far too much. If I let you, you'll go anywhere with them. That's why you're so lost right now."

This took his breath away. She saw to the depths of his dilemma with clarity far beyond his expectations. Was he that obvious? But he soon realized that wasn't all of it—this was proof. Proof of how closely this girl had been watching him.

"The strength of that curse must be captivating. I know—during the fight in the trunk, even from a distance, I could see how happy you looked. Delighted to fight right there with Mr. Horn and Ms. Hibiya. Even if the price was this terrifying curse eating away at you."

"___!"

He could think of no rebuttals. Like Rita mentioned, those were the exact emotions that had won out—and they were still smoldering away within. That was why he was hesitant to return the curse to Baldia. And Rita had been there for it. She'd seen it happen, so how could he attempt to explain it away?

"...You don't have a fighter's nature," Rita told him. "You were built to cultivate—not destroy and slaughter. But becoming a wrangler changes that. Takes that same talent and turns it to death and devastation. In exchange for all the beautiful things those hands could have grown."

Rita's voice was shaking. Guy could tell this was what she feared most. Only now was he realizing this wasn't an issue for the Sword Roses alone. This was a huge decision. It would affect any number of lives—and vastly change some of them.

"Maybe that'll do it for you," Rita added. "If you can be with the Sword Roses, protect them with your own hands—then perhaps the price will be worth it. But I can't bear the thought. I can't, and I won't. I don't want to lose you. You belong in the sun, with a smile on your face...!"

Her words were almost a shriek now. Guy was way past asking anything stupid like *Why?* He'd felt it himself any number of times, unrelated to Rita. In an unnatural environment like Kimberly, someone like him stood out all the more. Perhaps on a smaller scale than Purgatory—Alvin Godfrey—but both had been adored for the same reason.

Rita wiped her tears and put her hands to her breast. She looked Guy in the eye once again, not letting him take a turn. She'd come here prepared for every step of this, but his heart was not ready for anything. All he could do was stand there like a stick of wood, hearing her words, incapable of anything more.

"I'll care for the plants you left in the conservatory. You don't mind, right? I often joined you in making observations, so it'll be easier for me to take over. And you won't owe any upperclassmen anything."

"...I'd...appreciate that. But...Rita..."

"You won't owe me. Just...come see me. Once every few days—or even once a week. I'll give you a progress update on the plants. It won't take that long."

She wasn't backing down. His feeble efforts to throw a wrench in her plans were in vain—her strength of will batted it away. Rita was hardly in her right mind. She'd chosen to unleash it all here, which was why no modest effort would stop her. Cheeks flushed with excitement and shame, the tremor in her voice growing stronger, she pressed on.

"A-and if you feel a need for human warmth, go right ahead. I-it's not like my body's a turnoff for you, is it? I heard you talking about your type. You like big, strong gals, even if they're a bit awkward—I was so relieved to hear that. I got quite carried away, feeling like I had at least one thing you would like."

A painful confession that made him downright dizzy. Objectively speaking, Rita was certainly taller than average, but not in any way awkward. And mages were capable of adjusting their figure by hook or by crook, yet she always put herself down for the simple reason that the root of her self-loathing ran far deeper—and he'd just caught a glimpse of it. Her nails dug into her chest, as if she'd read his mind.

"I knew you wouldn't recoil from this! That's why I fell for you; that's why I knew I could give myself to you. This isn't nearly as infectious as that curse—and if I'm aware of the risks and take measures, yours won't transfer that easily, either. So if you want me, just...say the word. I have no experience, but...I'll do anything I can."

Too worked up to hide her feelings anymore, Rita buried her face in both hands. Guy wanted to abandon words, pull her close, rub her head—and once she'd calmed down, chew her out for several hours. But now that wasn't an option. No matter how much she begged for it, he couldn't take her up on the offer. Helpless, Guy gnashed his teeth and managed a feeble response.

"...Man, I'd love to give you a piece of my mind, but...the words ain't coming. It's too much at once, I guess. You couldn't have doled this out a bit at a time?"

"...Sorry. If I'm honest, I wanted to leave your head spinning. If I wore you out...maybe you'd let me slip in."

She could have easily left that unsaid. But she didn't have the nerve to share her feelings with ulterior motives unspoken; that awkward honesty made him care all the more.

At last, his emotions fell in line. He took a few breaths and began to sort himself out. More than anything, this was hardly an issue that came down to a yes or no. This was something they had to work themselves up to, look each other in the eye, and discuss over time. Not a process that could begin right here. So the first thing he needed to tell her was that he wanted to do just that.

"...Give me time. I can't say anything here and now. Once my head's cooled off, maybe I can scold you properly."

"...Okay. I'll...be waiting for that."

Rita got it. She pulled her hands from her flushed face, looking up at him with expectation and anxiety in equal measures. Guy winced. For all her bold moves, he knew this had taken a lot of courage.

"...Um, so...can I handle your plants?"

She barely got the question out. Whatever came of the rest—that much, she wanted to nail down. Sensing that, Guy folded his arms, looking her over.

"If I say no, you'll take it as rejection. I ain't letting you off the hook that easy. You'd better cultivate 'em properly! You let a single one wilt, I'll be hopping mad."

"Got it! I promise—they're in good hands!"

Rita nodded, tears in her eyes. Guy grinned, nodded, and waved as he moved past her.

Whatever happened, he was a long way from rejoining the Sword Roses. Maybe it wouldn't be a bad idea to take care of some other stuff in the meanwhile. That was about as positive as he could get right now.

Once Guy vanished around the bend, Rita took her sweet time settling herself down. Then a thought struck her, and she called out to the silence.

"......Are you there, Teresa?"

Her voice echoed through the empty hall. Rita didn't bother looking around—she knew that was futile. After a moment, a flat voice spoke right behind her.

"How'd you know?"

She turned to find her tiny friend standing there. Always one to pop up out of nowhere.

Rita shook her head. "I didn't. Not at all. Didn't see any signs. I just...had a hunch. Maybe you'd be worried enough to come check on me."

Pure instinct, merely a passing fancy. Being right this time didn't really change a thing. Teresa seemed unconvinced, but Rita knelt down, putting herself at the smaller girl's eye level.

"Sorry, did I upset you? But I've gotta make this play. What do you make of it, Teresa? Mr. Greenwood and Mr. Horn are both friends of yours, and here I am, trying to pry them apart. You heard what went down—are you still on my side?"

She held Teresa's gaze the whole time. Rita had no intention of letting this go unsaid or obfuscated. When she'd decided to head into the lava tree mold, this girl had been the first friend to back her reckless plan. This could well be taken as a violation of that trust. If so, there was little she could do—but at the very least, Rita did not want to coat it in a lie.

Teresa stared back at her in silence. That same expressionless mask she always wore. Yet—right now, Rita felt like she could see past it. She'd known this girl a long time. And she knew by this point the emotions bottled up inside Teresa Carste were as violent as the surface was calm.

"You're stuck between a rock and a hard place, huh? I get that," Rita said, putting her arms around that tiny frame. Teresa seemed flustered but accepted the embrace, and Rita whispered in her ear, "Thank you, Teresa."

"...For what?"

"For fretting over it. You could easily have just trimmed away anything that doesn't suit Mr. Horn's interests. But you aren't."

She buried her face in the girl's shoulders. Her friend was unable to choose, and that made her so happy, she could cry. This wasn't even a tough choice. Teresa merely needed to tell Mr. Horn everything, and that would be the end of it. No matter how she fought, if the Sword Roses closed ranks, her attempt would end there. Teresa had that card in her hand—and in her position, she should definitely play it.

So the fact that she was hesitating alone proved Rita had formed a real bond with Teresa. And she knew what a good friend she'd made, even if the path she was on might soon put an end to it.

"......"

Teresa's hand went around the back of Rita's hands and awkwardly stroked her friend's hair. She was not good at comfort or encouragement. But however paltry the effort, she felt the need to try. This was the first time she'd felt this impulse with anyone but Oliver or Shannon.

"I'll reserve judgment for now. We'd better get back to the Fellowship. Dean's running his mouth off; without you around, I'll be forced to duel him again."

"Okay. Sorry to ditch you there. Let's head back, Teresa."

Rita let go of her and held out a hand. Teresa took it, and they walked off together. Putting off the decision was neither wise nor practical. But it was a very human choice.

That same evening, Oliver and Nanao wrapped up classes a step ahead of the others and, as planned, headed to their hidden base. They had no other purpose than the desire to spend some time together—a minidate, essentially.

"I am at my wit's end. Never did I imagine I had left Dustin stewing like that," Nanao said after a sip of piping hot green tea.

The tea and brewing pot were gifts from Theodore's travels. Leaning back on the couch, Oliver waved a wand, pulling a plate of cookies from the shelf. Guy and Katie had baked them together; upon closer inspection, it was easy to tell who had shaped which cookie.

"In my eyes, it's no surprise," Oliver replied, taking a sip of his own tea. "With Ashbury gone, there's no broomrider on campus he's paid more attention to. He must have assumed you'd picked up on that, yet you didn't even pay him a visit."

Nanao shuddered, a guilty look on her face. "Then I am ashamed. I certainly knew he had a high opinion of me, but the rest escaped my notice. Not wanting to compound the issue, I have already completed the paperwork to join his seminar."

He blinked at her, slightly surprised. She'd already committed?

Oliver set his mug down. "Have you? Are you sure that's the right choice? Instructor Garland had his eye on you, too."

Just covering his bases. Nanao folded her arms, scowling.

"I am aware. But if I may speak from my gut, I feel he does not especially wish to be my mentor. He has voiced no objections, but he has kept his distance. 'Tis but a vague impression, yet he has consistently toed that line."

"...Oh...?"

Oliver considered that.

What could it mean? Garland was passionate about sword arts instruction, every bit as big on nurturing talent as Dustin was with broomriding. Oliver had just assumed he would be keen on making Nanao his apprentice. Garland's style was all about actively analyzing and breaking down the outstanding elements of other fighting schools, so what would make him want to avoid taking Nanao on?

As Oliver busied himself with these thoughts, Nanao finished her tea, put her mug down, and toppled over, her head on his lap. This did not surprise him in the least. Nanao was prone to these sudden affectionate gestures.

"Either way, I have escaped this conundrum. How fare you, Oliver? Will you be joining Katie at the place you visited?"

"...Up to her. But I'm thinking it's likely," he said, remembering how Katie had taken to it. "They made a good impression, and no other seminar is that tailored to her interests. She's struggling less with the choice and more with committing to it. I'm just waiting for her to say the word."

Nanao looked up at Oliver, her expression grave. "Glad to hear it. Do not take your eyes off her. Of course, I am watching as best I can—but with Guy's absence, she stands on shifting sand. If Chela was not taking a turn, I would not dare leave her side to join you here."

"Yeah, I know. If Guy comes back, we'll see some improvement, and I don't doubt he'll make that choice. My only concern is what form his return will take."

Nodding, he narrowed his eyes. This concern had stuck with him— Guy's default nature versus his aptitude for curse wrangling. Oliver knew his friend well enough to know just how hard a choice that would be.

"...*Fantastic,*" Guy had said. Laden with curses, painful to even look at—yet he'd been ecstatic.

Each time he remembered it, Oliver felt anguish and fear in equal measure. And it made him wonder—if Guy came back to them the way he expected, would that really be for the best?

Or was *he* dragging Guy down? Pulling a man meant to smile in the light down into darkness where Oliver himself dwelled? If Guy had never met the Sword Roses, would he even have considered becoming a wrangler?

Mostly likely not. It would not even have been a dilemma. Even if his talent was as exceptional as Zelma said, Guy would have shown no interest in pursuing that path. What he craved, what he was loath to relinquish was the power that came with it. Curses were merely a means to that end—all so he could stand with them and keep them safe.

"Yoink!"

His thoughts were interrupted by fingers pulling on each of his cheeks. Nanao had reached up to him. He blinked down at her, and she lay there protesting.

"You shoulder too much, Oliver. Share this burden with me."

"Uh, yeah, I intend to. Just…"

He scrambled to respond, and she let go of his cheeks, burying her face in his stomach. Her empty hand moved around his back, pulling him close, and her nose pressed up against him—sniffing him.

"…Ahh…"

A faint herbal fragrance teased her nostrils. She knew this was no cologne, but a scent generated by his body. And he had relayed the cause to her in bed with a sad smile:

"Ever since I was small, I've used powerful potions so frequently, it changed the very makeup of my body. Perhaps it's a bit like the scars you bear."

She'd always been fond of the scent, but that revelation made it all the more acute. She longed to bask in it forever, and smelling it alone was hardly enough.

Nanao increased the strength of her embrace, and sensing that mute request, Oliver asked, "…Do you want to, Nanao? Here, now?"

His fingers played with her hair, the nape of her neck. He already knew the answer to his question. Nanao peeled her face from his abdomen, looking up through her lashes.

"Desperately. Do you even realize it has been an entire week since we last indulged?"

"With Guy's mess in the middle—"

His excuses were silenced with a kiss. The astonishing heat of her lips momentarily eased all concerns occupying his mind. She'd been waiting for that, he realized, so he kissed her back with love and gratitude.

Every last nerve focused on their lips alone, the world around them melting away.

For a long moment, they remained like that, locked in an embrace, then his fingertips tapped Nanao's back. She blinked and peeled away. They were reflected in each other's eyes, awash with ardor and exaltation, a mere confirmation that the prelude was done.

But before they got down to business, a reminder—one Oliver barely managed to get out.

"...They'll be joining us in two hours. We can't exactly take our time."

"Then let us make up for it with vigor. Any requests?"

"Any number of them, but first—let's get you sated."

No further confirmations required—Oliver got to work. Time was limited, but some things could not be rushed. Mages paid no heed to wrinkled clothes, so Oliver didn't need to undress Nanao right away to hide the evidence. He applied stimulus in stages, an extension of standard healing: from her back to her sides, from her sides to her breasts— then a jump to her ears. No surprises there—this was a process they'd discovered together in their endeavors.

"...Mmff..."

As he nibbled on her earlobe, Nanao writhed, as ticklish as it was pleasurable. Not about to go down without a fight, she wrapped her lips around the side of his neck. Oliver's shoulder quivered, and a breath escaped him.

He could not let his guard down for a second. Nanao was never one to let him keep the lead. There were signs she viewed this as a contest to see which of them could get the other off first. Accepting her offensive, Oliver was obligated to maintain his own technical performance. This was easier said than done, but always fun. An extension of their usual play, the pleasure and safety of it always a comfort.

"___!"

But then some static interfered. Nanao's shirt unbuttoned, he parted the cloth, revealing a bra that Katie had likely chosen for her. His hands were around her back to unfasten it, but as her well-shaped breasts came into view, something flicked across his mind.

The events in his dorm, Pete waiting for him in girls' clothes, everything he'd said, the two options presented to Oliver, and, helpless to resist, their bodies mingling after. That had not been an isolated incident, and they still lay together.

Oliver's skin was not thick enough, nor was his mind nimble enough to put that all away and drown himself in Nanao alone.

"You are keeping secrets from me...?" Nanao whispered, surmising as much.

Oliver ceased all motion, freezing up. For a moment, he looked ready to cry. Anguished at his inability to share, his heart splitting with the urge to spill everything. He had to respond somehow. She'd asked, and he had to answer, but not a single word came to mind. He could not tell her, but his heart could not bear to paint it over with a coat of lies, even though he had done as much countless times before.

As he found himself trapped in a desperate corner, Nanao's finger pressed to Oliver's lips. He blinked, and she smiled pleasantly, like a calm ocean beneath a clear blue sky.

"Say not a word. I will not inquire. Since the moment we first met, your depths have been obscured—this is merely one more mystery they conceal."

With that, she put her arms around Oliver's head, not hesitating to pull him to her bare breasts. Wrapped in her soft flesh and warmth, comforted unconditionally, Oliver felt tears welling up in his eyes, and he could not stave off the sobs. Nanao accepted all of it, hugging him ever tighter.

"Whatever it is, I do not mind," she murmured. "That is but a piece of the man I love. Just...when you are ready, share it with me. Spare no thought to delicacy or fear."

He did not need to tell her, but he had permission to do so at any time. That was the one way she could offer him salvation. Arms

shaking, he managed to return the embrace. He longed to thank her, but that was beyond him now. He simply spoke her name, as if that said everything.

"...Nanao..."

"Mm, I am here. I am here for you, Oliver."

Her arms tightened around him again. Not poking his wounds, not even trying to locate them. Simply aligning herself with his pain— quietly, gently devoting herself to the boy she loved.

"Ow!"

A thrust to his chest sent Guy tumbling across the floor. He landed on his back, and a hand reached down to him.

"Sorry, too strong a hit. You okay?"

"Yeah, no prob. Appreciate you training with me."

Guy reached out and took the proffered hand. Gui Barthé pulled him up; they'd found an empty room to get some exercise in. Lélia Barthé was with them, reffing the match. And sitting in the corner, arms around one knee, a sullen look on her face, was Annie Mackley, dragged here against her will.

"I said to ask for anything, right? Sword practice doesn't even count. So I'm adding in some tips for free. I mean, your Lanoff's a mess, Greenwood."

Lélia's assessment was a candid one. Guy grimaced, raising his athame.

"Just call me Guy. But yeah, I figured as much. I ain't ever gonna be like Oliver," he muttered, naming his role model.

"I'm not suggesting you go crazy polishing yourself to his level." Lélia shrugged. "And if you aim to win by means other than the blade, fair enough. But if you are, then you oughtta focus on the techniques that buy you that time. You're strongest when you keep enough dis-tance to scatter toolplants, right?"

Her advice was tailored to him.

Guy tapped the ground with his toe. "If there's soil around, yeah. Fighting indoors like this, backing off ain't gonna do me a lick of good. I got real lucky with the terrain in the league and the lava tree mold. Fighting in regulation rings, my skills are bottom of the middle at best."

"Heh, how very you. Did you forget who mentored you? The one and only Survivor! To my knowledge, he never even tried to enter the combat league. But no one was better at navigating the labyrinth—even the school's biggest names respected him. It's all about how you use what you got. And are you even interested in picking fights and notching up victories?"

Lélia addressed the fundamental concern, and Guy sighed, sheathing his athame.

"Well, no. I came to Kimberly to study ancient and extinct species, but I'm better suited to growing crops down home on the farm. But that ain't my friends. They've been through some tough spots, and I know there's more of that coming. Katie and Pete are out there polishing their skills and getting stronger; I can't be left be—"

"They aren't right for you."

A voice cut him off. Flinching, Guy turned toward it. Mackley had held her tongue this whole time, but now she was scowling at him.

Her words were lost on him, so he asked, "What, Mackley? What do you mean?"

"What I said. You aren't like your friends. From what you're saying, you're after strength to keep them safe? That's all fine and dandy. But it's got jack shit to do with the path of your spell."

Mackley wasn't mincing words at all—and Guy couldn't immediately respond. Surprised to find he couldn't just laugh it off, he crossed his arms.

"...Uh...that's not true. They've all helped me study, helped with my research. And thanks to them, I've had a labyrinth workshop since year one."

"And in return, you damn near died how many times? Again, fine.

Suit yourself. But what, a labyrinth workshop? You still need that? You're about to join a seminar, get free use of their facilities. No need to be in the labyrinth—make a new workshop with students in your field. You're long past the need to be hung up on the shared base you prepped in the lower forms."

"...No, I'm..."

Mackley wasn't letting him get a word in edgewise. The more she spoke, the more worked up she got—without really realizing it. And having failed to stop herself, she'd gone past *voicing an opinion* and into *winding him up*.

"And helping with your research? You gonna pay for that with your life? That's a lousy deal by any standard. Ha-ha, your buddies sure know how to wheel and deal. I guess you can't put a price on friendship! They're really getting their money's worth. A beautiful bit of logic that lets them bleed you dry indefinitely."

"Okay, Mackley, that's enough," Gui said, deciding it was time to step in.

Catching herself, she awkwardly looked away, saying nothing else.

"You just have to say what everyone else is scared to, huh?" Gui sighed. "Good way to make enemies. You gotta build up to things! What good will it do to decide you'll piss him off anyway, so you might as well not hold back? You weren't trying to pick a fight with him, were you?"

"...Hmph..."

Mackley buried her face in her knees. Gui snorted at her, then turned toward Guy.

"Mackley massively overstated things. My sister and I agree on that. But—not everything she said is off base. Mind if I try translating the salient parts?"

"...Uh, sure, please," Guy said. He nodded, trying to stop his head from spinning.

Gui closed his eyes, picking his words.

"Simply put—you may have some blinders on. I get wanting to fight alongside your friends, but that's because Hibiya and the rest keep plunging headlong into danger. It's not what you actually wanna do. There's value in trimming that away and reevaluating. We may be stuck with our lot in life, but *you're* free to make some changes."

"...Trimming?" Guy frowned.

Gui shook his head. "Don't get me wrong, I'm not saying to cut them loose. Does it sound better if I call it 'adjusting your distance'? You've been tight with them since day one. I was with my sister and Lady Ursule before we got here, so I can only imagine, but making friends early on is critical to keeping yourself safe here. But not many people in the upper forms are still with the group they started out with. As they move up, they figure out what they're each good at, and their paths diverge. It's the natural result of finding what's best for yourself—and not in any way a bad thing."

Guy was taking his time, step by step, mindful of the logic. There was common ground in what they said, but this made a very different impression than Mackley's outburst. Without his feathers ruffled, it was hard to ignore the point. Seeing that on Guy's face, Lélia chimed in.

"You're in a different position than you were in year one. You've got knowledge and power, you've built a reputation on campus, and there are teachers and upperclassmen with their eye on you. Worst-case scenario, if you distance yourself from Horn and the others, you won't be alone. That much is an actual fact. At the very least, we're—"

"What a fascinating conversation!" a harsh new voice cut in.

His wand had cast amplification and convergence spells to make his words penetrate the sound-dampening barrier. Everyone gulped when they recognized the voice and turned toward the door, where a smaller boy stood, arms crossed. A bespectacled fourth-year reversi with a high-strung air about him—Pete Reston.

"Reston?!"

"How—?! We were soundproof!"

"You think that's foolproof, too? You think I'd let Guy roam free in this state?"

Pete's entrance had left Guy flat-footed, but this made him gasp. He started patting the pockets of his robe and soon found it: a coin-sized scout golem inside the hood. It had picked up their entire conversation and broadcast it via a mana frequency to Pete. Since the sound itself wasn't sent, the sound-dampening barrier couldn't stop it. Guy looked rather ill.

"......!"

"You've got a lotta nerve. You survived that mess through sheer luck, and a minute later, you're trying to poach him? Ha-ha, I'm amazed you thought you could get away with it. I thought everyone in our year knew just what fate lies in store for anyone who fucks with us."

Pete was stalking across the room, muttering. Clearly way past angry. Gui braced himself, Mackley put her back to the wall, and Lélia stepped out before them, hands up.

"Calm down, Reston! I know it sounded bad, but that wasn't our intent! We were just discussing possible futures for Guy. If you take offense to that advice, my brother and I will happily apologize. We have no intention of opposing you—"

"'Guy,' is it? Gosh, I had no idea you were on a first-name basis. Didn't expect you to work your wiles on him. Gotta raise my estimation of you. I only ever saw you as Valois's puppets before."

Lélia's defense backfired. As tensions mounted, Guy slammed the scout golem to the ground, closing in on Pete.

"Dammit, Pete...! Have you lost your mind? You've definitely got the wrong idea. We're just talking. They're not poaching me. I asked them to—"

The moment Guy was in range, Pete's arm went around the back of his head, yanking him in. Without a moment's hesitation, his lips were on Guy's. Something small slipped into Guy's mouth—a capsule of potion Pete had kept tucked in his cheek. It broke, and the fast-acting paralytic inside took control. When Guy's knees buckled, Pete caught him, lowering his friend to the floor with a grim smile.

"You shut up, Guy. This is on me—I should have forced myself on you long before this happened. I'm still far too *nice*. Even though I know the more stakes you pound, the better."

Rebuking himself, Pete drew his athame.

Some curse energy had transferred to him on that kiss, but Pete had prepped, and Guy had fought to stop it—the influence wasn't too dire. Pete was good to throw down. Seeing how ready he was, Lélia and Gui gave up and drew their own weapons.

"You're past letting us talk, huh? We're doing this right here? I don't recommend it. We'll be forced to defend ourselves—and it's three against one," said Lélia.

"...Huh? Wait, don't drag me into— Kah!"

Trying her best to stay plastered to the wall, Mackley let out a squawk, and her legs crumpled beneath her. The Barthés gasped.

"Now it's two-on-one. How dumb can you be? You seriously thought I'd roll up against these odds without a plan?"

Pete's lips twisted in a sneer. Sensing something closing in all around, Lélia cast a spell, illuminating her surroundings and shattering the visual illusion. That revealed the six-legged insectoid golems, about as big as midsize dog. They were everywhere: on the floor, on the ceiling, on the walls—over a dozen golems. A terrifying sight.

"Stealth golems!"

"...We're surrounded. When did he—?"

Cursing their lack of precautions, the Barthés put their backs together, athames raised. The surprise attack had them down a fighter, and now he had familiars—if they all attacked at once, Pete would have a huge advantage. Well aware of that, he raised his blade.

"I don't want to draw a crowd, so I'll make it quick. I'm gonna carve this lesson into you. Don't mess with the Sword Roses—!"

"Okay, Pete, time-out."

Just before he let loose, a breezy voice put him in a shoulderlock.

Pete flinched and turned to look at the intruder—a boy a head taller than him, Tullio Rossi.

"…?! Rossi…!"

"You are popping off! I 'ave to admit, they gave you good cause. We all 'ate 'aving those we adore snatched away, no? You more than the rest of us!"

Rossi was both sympathizing with and pinning Pete down. Not only was Pete's dominant athame hand in Rossi's clutches, but the Ytallian also wasn't letting him move a finger on his other hand, preventing him using any of the magic tools he had up his sleeve. Rossi knew full well Pete kept a whole bag of tricks on him, so he was shutting those options down. And running his mouth off the whole time.

"But going full terror on them right off the bat? I 'eard only the last exchange, but I feel they meant no 'arm. Objectively, you seriously think *the* Valois would even consider scouting Guy? I am sure this was just a passionate discussion of life's many tapestries that 'appened to strike a nerve. An unfortunate disconnect, eh?"

Despite Rossi's attempts at persuasion, the murderous fury radiating off Pete showed no signs of subsiding. Worst-case scenario, Rossi might have to knock the reversi out, but that might leave Rossi himself with a target on his back. As he weighed his options, a big man strode in.

"You're drunk on the power you've gained. Acting like a mage is all well and good, but the old you had his virtues. Wouldn't recommend taking it to extremes, Reston."

"…You too, Albright?"

Joseph Albright loomed over Pete, who ground his teeth.

"I rather like the new you," Rossi whispered in Pete's ear. "You 'ave seen what you want, and you are going for it—nothing wrong with that. Yet, I will say—do not forget the larger picture. Valois is slowly opening 'erself up to Nanao, yes? If you torture 'er servants, that will all be for naught. I am betting you forgot about that, no?"

"___!"

Eyes widening, Pete stopped struggling. Sensing this approach was getting through, Rossi pressed it. He released his grapple, neither wand nor blade in hand, bending a knee to put himself at the reversi's eye level.

"Much better. You 'ave a kind 'eart. It makes me want to put the moves on you. Would you care to 'ave tea? You would rather collect yourself before you go 'ome to Oliver, I am sure."

"...Shut up," Pete spat.

Rossi's breezy demeanor was slowly draining the tension from the room; paired with that reminder, it was effectively diminishing Pete's will to fight. He knew from experience how effectively this approach stifled impulsive conflicts. Though aware he was being manipulated, Pete was not dumb enough to buck against it for that reason alone. He took several deep breaths, letting his raging emotions vent, then glared back at the Barthé twins, who braced themselves.

"I'll let you off this time. Given my friend's work with Valois, I can't tell you to keep your distance from Guy, either. But just try and recommend he leave our group again—and I won't hesitate. You will suffer so much, you'll regret being born."

With that vehement threat, he spun around and stalked away, carrying Guy over one shoulder. Only when his footsteps vanished did Rossi let out a sigh of relief.

"...'Ow 'orrifying. The way 'e 'as grown—knowing 'im in 'is first year, I did not see this coming."

"Had he not changed, he'd be dead. But if he's sprouting horns, perhaps it's time we snapped one off," Albright muttered, staring after Pete.

Rossi turned his attention elsewhere. The Barthés had clearly not expected to be bailed out like this.

"A narrow escape, yes? I just 'appened to spot Pete sailing down the 'all, looking ready to commit murder. Turned to follow and thought it best to interfere. But 'onestly, you 'ave only yourselves to blame, no? What you tried 'ere was positively suicidal. Or did Oliver's and

Nanao's genteel dispositions give you the wrong idea?" Rossi asked. "The Sword Roses are our year's greatest threat, and every member is a ticking time bomb of a mage. Meddle with them foolishly, and you are liable to wind up dead. Even if you mean well."

This was as serious as Rossi had ever looked, and Lélia and Gui each put their blades away, taking it to heart.

"...Message received. But we're in the position we're in—and we owe him a debt."

"Yeah, can't exactly get cold feet that easily."

Rossi blinked, as if he had not expected them to stand their ground. "My, look at the both of you. Not long ago, you might as well 'ave been storefront mannequins. Is this Guy's influence? That man cannot be underestimated."

With that, he spun around and exited the room, Albright in tow. The Barthés exchanged a look.

"...That was too close," Gui said. "What now?"

"Is it even worth considering? If his friends are in that frame of mind, all the more reason Guy needs to hear outside perspectives. But I'm not about to ruffle Reston's feathers any further. We'll need a better approach. Lay the groundwork before we hit the man himself? I doubt the other Sword Roses are *that* intense about it..."

Lélia trailed off in thought, chin in hand. But then a feeble voice came from the back wall, reminding them they were not alone.

"...Hey...if it's over...help me up..."

Mackley had been taken out quick but was still with them—and they rushed to her aide.

"Sorry, Mackley. Totally forgot about you."

"You really got the short end of the stick. But you know the old saying—loose lips sink ships."

"You're the ones who dragged me in here!" she yelled as loudly as her paralyzed vocal cords let her. It took the Barthés far longer to soothe her ruffled feathers than it did to undo the paralysis.

*   *   *

With Guy still unable to move, Pete brought him out of the building to the fountain square by their dorms and dropped him on a bench there. Pete had been carrying a boy far bulkier than himself but wasn't even out of breath—proof he'd learned to channel his mana into his physical exertions.

"...Urgh..."

"Sorry to force the issue. The paralysis should be wearing off. Tell me when you're ready—I'd appreciate you taking this curse back off me," Pete said as he settled down on the bench next to Guy.

Pete's face and tone were totally lacking the edge he'd had against the Barthés. He was only like this with his friends. All his hatred pointed outward, all his love inward. Even if those boundaries were not so easily drawn, this was Pete's fundamental emotional state.

Smiling at his friend, Pete waited for Guy's next move. But though the paralysis had long since worn off, Guy said not a word, just sitting there and staring at him.

"What?" Pete said, disgruntled. "We can make out if you want."

"...So you aren't joking about that, huh?" Guy muttered, leaning back against the bench.

"You thought I was?" Pete looked offended. "I've been dead serious since I first mentioned it. Not just you, either—I want the closest ties I can get to every member of the Sword Roses. Leave myself options for when I have a kid with someone. I've got no reservations about doing that with any of you."

His position felt awfully extreme, and Guy rubbed his temples.

"When'd you get this far gone? Was what we had not enough?"

"Nope. Far too unstable for my needs. I want a rose where the petals will never scatter. I want to make that moment last forever."

Pete's eyes were on the night sky. Guy remembered their visit to Pete's home, and he couldn't deny this impulse outright. He had many a gripe about the means to that end but knew arguing about those was the last thing Pete needed now.

The right choice was clear. First, meet him halfway, pull his tiny frame in close. Prove the love and warmth within Guy had not gone anywhere. And yet, that was the one thing Guy could not do right now. A painful reminder of that fact, it cut him to the quick—and his next breath was nearly a sob.

"...Fuck, this again? Can't even slap you, much less give you a hug."

"Go right ahead. Instructor Zelma said what she had to, but you know a curse won't attach itself from one or two transmissions. Even if there's some minor side effects, I'll deal with it. If it's for your sake."

Pete offered a soft smile—as warm as the flinty gaze he directed at his enemies was cold. Guy could tell this was what came naturally to Pete. Here was someone who picked his family and gave them all his love, protection, and affection. The line between in and out was far stronger than Guy's own, so perhaps it was inevitable his approach was both possessive and rejective.

Guy weakly reached out, lightly touched Pete's shoulder, and took back the curse energy that had been transmitted orally. He soon pulled away again, and Pete pursed his lips, dissatisfied.

"What, no more kissing? You're an incorrigible tease."

"...I'm actually gonna get mad, y'know."

"Don't. That one was a joke," Pete told him. "Good night, Guy. Shame I can't get a good night hug, but I'll take a rain check."

Pete stood up and headed toward the dorm. Too weak to follow, Guy watched him go, feeling so helpless, he could cry.

"You deal with him every night, Oliver?" he muttered. "That's gotta be rough..."

Naturally, it *was* rough. No one was bearing the brunt of Pete's changes harder than his roommate. And nobody felt more obligated to deal with it head-on.

"Pete, we need to talk."

Oliver got back to their dorm an hour after Pete, well into the middle of the night. Seeing his friend still up, reading in bed, he figured this was the time.

"Why so formal, Oliver?" Pete said, closing the book with a smile. "Not feeling up to it tonight?"

"Not about that. You know what I mean. Don't play games. Albright briefed me. You nearly took out the Barthé twins for daring to speak with Guy?"

Oliver pushed past his friend's deflections, getting to the heart of the matter. He and Nanao had run into Albright on their return to campus and gotten up to speed. Pete snorted, figuring that was Oliver's source.

"Knew he'd snitch. But yeah, it's true. They sounded like they were trying to pry Guy away from us, so I gave them a little warning. Can't believe anyone still takes us that lightly."

"I doubt that's the truth. Given their standing, they wouldn't be trying to poach him. They were just discussing possibilities. You were eavesdropping and overreacted. And you know it."

Oliver was quite sure of himself. The way Pete had been acting lately, it was only a matter of time before he bumped antlers with someone somewhere. On the receiving end of Oliver's glare, Pete didn't bat an eye.

"Maybe. But does that really matter? It's a critical juncture for him; anyone saying the wrong thing at a time like this deserves some backlash. I'd rather overreact like this and scare people off than risk overlooking a legit attempt and losing Guy to it. Make an example of 'em," Pete said, then added with a sigh, "Though, I got interrupted this time."

Rubbing his brow, Oliver hung his head. Pete's position was far more intractable than he'd hoped.

"The way you think is way past 'friendship.' Even allowing for this being Kimberly. Guy saved the Barthés, and that made them closer.

This is a connection Guy earned himself through his actions in the lava tree mold. Did you not consider how your choices might have cost him that?"

"Sure, maybe he'll lose a few connections. But I'll make that up to him. Find him some friends that get our deal and don't run their damn mouths off. Don't get the wrong idea—I'm not objecting to Guy having friends outside our group. I'm just batting away the pests. If we don't, they'll only start siphoning away his nectar."

Pete was shrugging this off like it was normal, and Oliver clenched his fists. By what criteria was Pete separating "pests" from the rest? If that included everything Guy took an interest in outside the Sword Roses, then that would be no better than shackles around his limbs. Pete himself insisted otherwise, but the instant the measure of it lay in Pete's subjective scales, it was already wrong.

Yet, at the same time, Oliver understood that Pete's sense of what was normal was growing ever hazier. Becoming more of a mage, acquiring more techniques—one's perspective on the world was bound to shift. He'd learned just how far his hands could reach. Living as an ordinary had made the hearts of others an insurmountable challenge. But not anymore. Everything he'd learned here gave him the means to meddle. And even in the magical world, reversis were rare. If he polished his charm techniques, he could entice mages of any gender.

"Please, Pete. Let my words sink in. You don't need to be so high-strung—Guy's not gonna leave us that easy. Miligan was right about that. If you have faith in him, you'll know you don't need to build walls. Katie's just as anxious, but she's pulling it off—"

As he pleaded, Oliver moved over to Pete's bed. Pete got up, snuggling against his chest. He closed his eyes and smiled.

"Enough, Oliver. You've made your point, and I've heard it. I definitely acted without considering Nanao's efforts with Valois. I'll pick an approach that won't cause such frictions next time. Deal?"

"Wait, Pete, that's not even my point—"

Sensing the topic drifting away, Oliver tried to steer it back—but

Pete's lips sealed his, just as Nanao's had earlier that evening. The fact that Oliver was doing this again before the date even changed made him shudder—and Pete only pulled away when he was sure Oliver had been silenced.

"I don't mind you lecturing me. You're always so earnest about it, and that makes me feel loved. But today, I'd rather be comforted. Being with Guy, unable to touch him—it was pretty hard to bear. I'm frustrated! If it wasn't for that curse, we could have pulled him into a threesome."

"......!"

Oliver couldn't believe his ears. Even Pete's admissions of fragility were laced with an edge of something frightening. He could tell Pete genuinely regretted not being able to make that threesome happen, and Pete would have said exactly the same thing if Guy was here with them. His smile would not have changed with more members in their tryst; his only concern was how to love them all at once. In Pete's mind, there was no contradiction there.

The kiss over, Pete went back to hugging. His face buried in Oliver's shirt, sniffing him—verifying the lingering fragrance he'd noticed on their first embrace. Sure of it, he smirked up at Oliver.

"Oh, you were with Nanao before? So you're not the least bit pent-up. Heh-heh... She beat me to the punch. Guess we'll have to take it nice and slow."

"Wait...Pete, wait..."

Oliver was pulled into bed, his protests in vain. His robe was stripped off, his buttons undone, and Pete's fingers slid into his open shirtfront. Pete's foreplay skills were getting better daily, and Oliver let out a moan, his rational mind slipping away.

How did we end up like this? The act itself is one thing; I can't refuse you, so I've accepted that. But I'd like to talk to you first. To fully understand the scent of danger I'm getting from you. To consider together how you should proceed. That's really all I want.

"...Pete...!!"

"Eep?!"

The panic and grief building up within had burst. Oliver's hands went around Pete's back, locking onto his erogenous zones, pressing hard into his skin, and doubling the mana flow with pinpoint accuracy. Pete's body jumped, and his offensive faltered; Oliver pressed the advantage, turning the tables, getting his hands all over him. Silencing Pete's resistance with a kiss, he peeled his clothes away so fast, he nearly took the skin with them, then he wet a finger with saliva and excavated Pete's navel with it. The mana stimulation flowing there was the last straw, and the overwhelming surge of pleasure rising up within swallowed Pete whole.

"Ah...! Wh-where's this coming from, Oliver? You're not usually so force— Hnahhhh!"

He wasn't about to give Pete enough leeway to offer feedback. Generally, Oliver took his sweet time working up to things, but there were no such considerations today. He was going for maximum effectiveness, starting an avalanche of pleasure—and keeping him there. Applying healing principles to heavy petting was Oliver's field of expertise, and however quick he'd learned, Pete was still nowhere near his level. And thus, when Oliver meant business, Pete was left writhing helplessly in bed.

"S-stop! Hold up, Oliver! Gimme a second to—"

"...You didn't wait for me," Oliver muttered, tears in his eyes.

Even as he spoke, his fingers were still prodding Pete's known weak points. Pete's back arced like a bow, past the point of speech, but that act played into Oliver's hands, too. The stimulation was far too intense, the pleasure way too strong—Pete's mind went blank.

"Ahh—"

And as the orgasm took hold, the vital restraints within, long since straining, gave way. The blood drained from his slack features, he shoved Oliver away with both hands, scrabbling at the sheets. Curling up in the corner, arms clutched to his chest, quivering in silence.

"...Pete?"

Baffled by this unexpected response, Oliver moved close on one knee—and then the process started. A faint glow surrounded Pete, and within that mystic light, his very figure transformed. His shoulders broadened slightly, and the two mounds on his chest subsided; his body was rapidly switching to his other polarity.

"——?!"

"...I said...stop..." Pete sobbed, mid-change.

Oliver watched, stunned. It was over in mere minutes. Pete had remained small of stature, so the difference was not readily apparent. Yet, what had happened was clear. The faint trace of mana each mage's body perpetually gave off bore a distinct signature, and generally, that changed so little, other mages could identify one another by it. But Pete's signature was markedly different from a moment ago. Not something possible if the nature of the change had only affected his exterior.

"...Per the phases of the moon, I'd normally lean male right now," Pete confessed, his voice barely audible. "I've been keeping myself female through sheer self-control. I didn't mention it, but...for a while now..."

This was a surprise to Oliver. He *had* noticed Pete had been female for some time; as Pete acclimated to the whole reversi thing, he'd learned to pick his form at will. But that did not mean he could entirely ignore the natural reversi cycle. Oliver himself had no first-hand experience with the difficulties of resisting that, but it was not hard to imagine the toll was considerable.

"...Why force yourself...?" he asked Pete.

"Because I wanted to do this with you, obviously!"

Pete's cry was choked with tears, his back turned adamantly away. And that gouged a deep hole in Oliver's chest.

What a foolish thing to ask. That had likely been the most tactless response imaginable—he regretted it deeply. He should have known better. If no one else, Oliver alone should have immediately grasped this cause.

"I take that back, Pete. Please...won't you turn and face me?"

His apology emotional, he pleaded with those delicate shoulders. Pete hesitated for a long, long time, and when he did turn, he was still trembling. His body was very much male.

"I would like to make this up to you. Shall we carry right along?"

"Huh—?"

Pete looked startled, but Oliver ran a hand down his side, making him jump.

"Eeek?! Wh-what are you doing? I'm a boy now…!"

"Honestly, I've never really minded that. You're *you*."

That came without hesitation. Oliver gently stroked Pete's bare skin, and each time, incredible pleasure shot up the reversi's spine. Before he knew it, Pete was pressed up against Oliver, moaning. Pete had yet to make love in this body, and each sensation it provided was terrifyingly novel. He'd unconsciously drawn a line, never asking for it in this form—but Oliver stepped right across that boundary.

"I'm more familiar with the workings here. It's actually easier," he whispered in Pete's ear. "Don't hold back—give yourself over to it. Today, *I* want to."

A shock ran down Pete's back. His hands and feet went limp—and no further thought was possible.

When they were done and had cleaned up, they shared a bed once more—this time for slumber. Now in their pajamas, they stared at each other.

"Sorry about that…," Pete murmured.

"Mm?" Oliver asked with a smile.

Pete looked away, embarrassed and awkward.

"This might sound like an excuse, but…I think the stress of suppressing the change had me pretty riled up. My head's cleared…now that I've turned male and…gotten some relief…"

The memories of that had him blushing again, and Oliver gently ran a finger down his cheek.

"And that's another way this affects you, huh? Sorry, I should have realized."

"Don't you dare. I may have been a tad eager, but even now, my core stance hasn't changed."

He reached out and gave Oliver a hug.

Pete had things he could not lose. He'd risk anything to keep them safe; his love was so great, he'd never let that go—even if it meant turning himself into something else.

"I'm not letting anyone have you. I'm not letting you go anywhere else. Not Guy, Katie, Nanao, Chela...or you...!"

A wish like a curse. Oliver had no words to respond to this, so he merely returned a silent embrace. It burned him to know this wish could not come to pass—and he was pushing Pete toward a corner with no escape.

CHAPTER 3

§

Tear

It was the morning after the tumultuous nighttime faculty meeting. Ted and Dustin were in the school building bright and early, awaiting a colleague's arrival.

"Ah, good morning, gentlemen."

Shortly before the real tide of students arrived—neither especially early nor late—Farquois strode in, hand raised to greet them. The great sage had raised their right hand, but the left—the one severed the day before—was back to normal, as if it had never been gone.

"...Too fast to rebuild an arm," Ted said, seeing through it. "That one's false?"

"Well, yes. Even here, the students would be shocked to see a teacher down a limb. Though, several spotted me on the way out."

They showed off their new arm, so well-made that the difference was not discernible at a glance. From the movement of the fingers, it was clear the limb was fully functional. There was no doubt that high-level golem techniques had been applied—but to the great sage, that was merely an exercise.

Seeing both Ted and Dusting sporting grim visages, Farquois flashed a smile.

"I caused you some concern, yes? But honestly, I did not expect you to defend me to such an extent. Especially you, Williams—why go out on a limb like that? You've been more guarded than anyone."

"...Even if I have, that doesn't mean we should go sowing the seeds of strife with the Gnostic Hunters. Do try to restrain yourself. She was not kidding about taking your head next time."

Ted issued this warning despite knowing it was likely futile.

"...Do those big shots at HQ want her gone that bad?" Dustin chimed in, scratching the back of his head.

"Ha-ha. Is it that obvious? Still, this is nothing new. Esmeralda's position has been too strong for too long, and if anything, she's only growing more powerful by the day. They'd love to pull the rug out from under her. Before she puts a stop to all such plans."

Farquois wasn't bothering to hide what lay behind their stay at Kimberly. Dustin hadn't expected them to be quite this forthcoming but was aware there was little use being secretive after that meeting. The great sage would likely commit themself to that role now, and thus, they had no reason to conceal a thing.

"Also, they harbor a deep-seated distrust toward her. And she *does* have a considerable appetite for tír research, yes?" Farquois offered. "The hurdles are high, but in no way has she forbidden students from tackling the subject. Just two years back, a student researching Luftmarz was quite dramatically consumed by the spell. And the fastest witch perished serving as his Final Visitor. Such a crying shame. If both had lived, they could have done much more."

Those events were still vivid in Dustin's mind. Ted had helped pull him out of his funk, but Ashbury's and Morgan's ends weighed heavily on him. Was there really no way to have avoided those deaths? The question haunted him. Farquois had called that a crying shame, which made it sound as if *they themself* could have saved both. That implication certainly ruffled Dustin, but the great sage did not dig that hole any deeper.

"The Five Rods are all about ostracism, so that subject rankles them. Studies within the Gnostic Hunters' headquarters are one thing, but they cannot abide an educational institute like Kimberly having free rein," said Farquois. "Still...Esmeralda has enough power to force the issue. It's the three faculty disappearances that painted a target on her back. Put the idea in their head that this is the time to drag her from her seat."

"...Do you agree with them? Since as you're here at the Five Rods' behest?"

Ted voiced the big question. Fully expecting it to be a mere confirmation. Instead...

"Do I?" Farquois asked, crooking their head. "I'm certainly against the school style, but to be frank, I really have no interest in such political shenanigans. I've taken the job—I'll perform it to their expectations. But I haven't really given much thought to anything beyond that. And I doubt Esmeralda's going to take their attempts lying down."

Irritated by this, Ted offered a rebuke. "...If that's no deception, then it's simply irresponsible. You've voluntarily stepped into a vortex that could shift the very power balance of the magical world. Yet, you care little for the outcome? I'll be honest, I find that highly doubtful. Hardly the words of a great sage."

Farquois shrugged. "That's the thing, isn't it?" they said. "I'm the great sage; I view these matters from an entirely different perspective. I do not expect to be understood. That hope, I abandoned long ago—but the reminder of it does bring a pang to my heart."

With that, their stalled feet moved again, signaling an end to the chat. Taking the hint, Ted and Dustin stepped aside, letting Farquois pass.

Then Farquois whispered, half to themself, "But perhaps someday, you'll catch up with me. Rest assured, I will pave a path in that direction."

"......?"

This was a different shade from any other utterance, underpinned by an uncanny gravitas. Ted could not tear his eyes off the great sage's back as they vanished around the bend. His impression of the mage was growing yet more enigmatic.

"...Can't get a read on them," he said, frowning. "What am I supposed to make of that remark?"

"Don't overthink it," Dustin advised. "That's what they want.

Still—they may mean it when they claim to have no real interest. They were never the political type. If they were so inclined, they would've long since been a member of the Five Rods."

Dustin refused to overcomplicate the issue. Just knowing that Farquois was acting on behalf of the Five Rods meant speculating on the mage's own motives was likely a fool's errand. Let the great sage's mind remain opaque—Dustin hailed from the Gnostic fronts and knew the Five Rods all too well.

"...Whose scenario is this? Hundred or Hook Nose are prone to such schemes, but this doesn't feel like their handiwork," said Dustin. "Arachne feels most likely... Alphonse? Lord, that man never changes."

"Mr. Walch? He once requested a potion from me. He seemed to be suffering. Unable to sleep, phantom pains from his missing half."

"Yeah, luck was against him, and the etheric body got torn away. No healing on earth will make it grow back. Still, ain't no reason to go crazy with it and add spider legs. Can't even walk down the street like that."

Dustin sighed, remembering his old war comrade.

Not just ordinary folk—most mages would find it hard to tell the difference between Gnostic Hunters and the monsters they fought. But spend time fighting alongside them, and that perspective changed forever. Dustin definitely knew what those people had thrown away to reach that state—and the painful void they could barely perceive.

"...The Five Rods are all like that. But I've risked my life in the field with every one of them. I'd rather not butt heads. Glad you spoke up, Ted."

"No, I feel much the same way. I got you and Isko mixed up in this alliance, so it's my role to put myself in the line of fire. At least, as long as my head remains on my shoulders."

"That's the spirit. The headmistress's blade moves at different speeds—whether it's your head or Farquois's doesn't matter. We gotta focus on getting through their term here. I'm far less concerned about what they get up to than whether the headmistress decides to take them down."

Dustin shifted gears to forthcoming prospects.

It seemed very likely that Farquois baiting Esmeralda into attacking them was all part of the Five Rods' plan. An awfully big piece to use as a sacrificial pawn, but if the great sage themself had fallen out of favor, it wasn't out of the question. Either way, the two of them need not dance to that tune.

"If nothing happens this year, I bet the Five Rods'll just claim dispatching Farquois ended the teacher disappearances. Let 'em. We can assume Instructor Theodore already has plenty of ammo ready to fight that sort of claim. We don't need to fuss about it."

"Appreciate you paring this mess down. Basically, all we have to do is ensure the great sage leaves here alive. That's our primary goal for the foreseeable future."

Dustin nodded at Ted's summation. He certainly had concerns about other factors that could worsen things, including whether the teacher killers would continue to target faculty under these conditions.

Turning back the clock to the night before—the Sherwoods had joined the Kimberly faculty by day, but in their hidden workshop in the labyrinth's first layer, they still held sway over their assembled comrades.

"Thank you for coming," Gwyn began. "Let's begin with news: We've figured out the general gist of why Farquois is here. This appears to be an attempt by the Gnostic Hunters to unseat the headmistress."

Gwyn got right down to business. Some were convinced, some confused. He elaborated:

"This is not merely circumstantial evidence; our comrades in the Gnostic Hunters backed it up. They've been plotting this for a while, and the teacher disappearances merely encouraged them to act. Clearly, the Five Rods loathe Esmeralda's influence more than we'd imagined."

"I figured as much."

"Not many other explanations."

Several comrades nodded. It went without speaking that anyone hoping to foster good relations with the headmistress would hardly send the great sage after her. Given the Gnostic Hunters' motivations, Gwyn turned his comments to how this affected their own actions.

"This is hardly as simple as 'the enemy of our enemy is our friend.' But we can look at it as a wind in our favor. Should they actually succeed in unseating Esmeralda, there'd be staff changes to follow—and that might give us the opportunity we seek. And we can take advantage of the chaos leading up to it. But it may also put avenging Lady Chloe further out of reach."

This last sentence was largely a consideration directed as his cousin, and Oliver expressed no dissatisfaction. When vengeance and their mission aligned, they would do anything to achieve it, but if the two purposes diverged, the latter was the natural priority. This was clear for all comrades, not just Oliver—a core belief that never wavered.

"That's sounding pretty optimistic. You think the headmistress is gonna let that happen? I'm betting we see a whole new set of Five Rods instead," said one comrade.

"But we're talking about how *we* should proceed," offered another. "Forget who'll win this political struggle—if the Gnostic Hunters thin our enemy's numbers, that's great for us. They already got Instructors Vanessa and Baldia pulled off campus. If we can count on that in the future, no harm backing them."

Opinions flew fast and furious, and Gwyn's eyes swept the table.

"Here's where I'm hoping for more perspectives. Our moles claim the Five Rods are dead set on the idea the disappearances are caused by an internal rift in the faculty. They're going after the headmistress for failing to mediate that. Farquois's purpose is to find evidence of the conflict or make it seem like their posting put an end to it."

Everyone crossed their arms, thinking. The Five Rods' take was wrong, but they knew exactly why. Three great mages slain—most would assume whoever achieved that was of equal or greater strength. Their own efforts to disguise the truth had directly led to that conclusion.

"If they're convinced it's a falling-out, they *would* take that approach. Everyone knows the great sage has the Gnostic Hunters' backing; them wandering around campus alone would make anyone think twice. If nothing else happens for a full year, people would give them credit for it. Which naturally lowers confidence in the headmistress and makes it easier to pin this on her."

"And if she beheads Farquois, all the better. The Gnostic Hunters sent them here to perform an inspection—their death would be justification for exacting payback. But the great sage ain't exactly suicidal. Not that you'd know it looking at the shit they've pulled since they got here."

"The way they're prancing, it's a wonder they aren't dead already. Hard to get a read on them, but I get the sense they're planning on garnering as much student-body support as they can while they're here? The Farquois faction's rising fast in the lower forms. Partially our fault for spending three years making this place feel even more dangerous."

There was a touch of self-rebuke in those words.

Once the stream of opinions died away, Gwyn moved things along.

"Either way, Farquois's behavior largely plays into our plans. I'm thinking we leave them alone for a while. We can always target a fourth afterward."

A concrete suggestion, and unsurprisingly, no one argued the point.

"Instructors Vanessa and Baldia are off at the front. Instructor Baldia might pop back in every now and then, but on her own terms; we can't plan for it. If we targeted anyone this year…"

"It would be Instructor Gilchrist or the headmistress herself. Honestly, I don't think we've got the forces for either. We haven't even filled in the losses from the Instructor Demitrio fight, and we've got a wild card like Farquois in the mix. Things might improve in the back half of this year, but—I still say we should take a full year off."

Silence signaled consensus; the final decision fell to their lord, Oliver. His comrades' eyes turned to him, and he took a moment to think before nodding gravely.

"...Very well. I agree it's too early to discuss plans for a fourth target. But if we are going to pin our hopes on Farquois, we will need a better grasp of their character. A pawn of the Five Rods meant to discredit Esmeralda—is that really all they are?"

He accepted the direction but focused on a doubt that was lodged deep in his mind. His comrades exchanged glances. This had clearly bothered them, too.

"They're a complete enigma," one comrade said. "It's been bugging me like crazy how unrelated their expressed views are to the Gnostic Hunter ethos. They're out here openly criticizing Kimberly's style, arguing in favor of prioritizing student safety... Isn't that, like...?"

"Civil rights movement thinking?" someone cut in, jumping ahead.

And that put identical grimaces on every face.

"Rod Farquois, *the* great sage? If that was true, it'd be *wild*. Put a tear in the eye of everyone at Featherston."

"It's a sick joke. Gotta be a performance designed to attract student support."

"But they're putting their neck out there, which is fascinating. You heard they came out of the meeting room down an arm. Rumor has it the headmistress called that punishment for their transgressions. They're way out on a limb—would not have surprised anyone if that had been their head instead."

Oliver's comrades seemed equally impressed and appalled. He was as well.

And that's what bugged him. If the great sage was just here to topple the headmistress per the Five Rods' plans, there was no need to attract this much attention. They'd be better off dutifully sticking to a substitute teacher's role. If the headmistress did cut them down, the Gnostic Hunters would use that as an excuse for retribution, but that was hardly the outcome Farquois themself was gunning for. In which case, this behavior must be to a purpose unrelated to that of the Five Rods.

"You believe we should step closer and attempt a deeper analysis, Noll?" Gwyn asked.

"Yes, Brother. Watching them unsettles me. But I cannot yet tell if that is good or bad."

A vague sensation at best. However, the most vivid image in his mind was how the great sage had held Lombardi's corpse in the lava tree mold trunk. If that had merely been a performance, it would not have stuck with him. And if was no act, then—

"Observations from a distance are getting us nowhere. Mindful of the risks of their charm, I'm going to attempt a face-to-face conversation with them," said Oliver. "I don't think that'll let me see what they're really thinking, but if I strike them from a new angle, I may catch a different ring."

Better to shun subterfuge, Oliver thought. Farquois was likely far better at that sort of thing—and it wasn't as if Oliver lacked excuses for a chat. As long as they were a teacher and he a student, interactions were a given.

"May I ask for some Wall Walking pointers, Instructor Farquois?"

Astrology class had ended, and he'd followed them into the hall.

At Oliver's call, the great sage glanced back at him. "Yes, certainly. Follow me."

With that, they walked off. Faintly surprised, Oliver followed.

"Now? If it's not a good time, I can wait…"

"No need. At your level, I'm confident this will not take long."

As they spoke, Farquois put a leg on a nearby windowsill, walking straight up the wall outside. Realizing the lesson had already begun, Oliver took his wand in hand, gathering himself—and stepped through the window as well. The great sage stopped a few steps above, looking down at Oliver's approach.

"At your age, merely standing and stopping on a wall is more than enough. Though clearly, that's hardly unusual at Kimberly."

"Yes, all the upperclassmen can do that much. If I can ask, when did you acquire the skill?"

"Me? When I emerged from my mother's womb. I stood right up and walked onto the ceiling—and only then did I let out my birthing cry."

Farquois spun around, walking off across the wall. Oliver tagged along, matching their pace, suppressing a sigh. Part of him would not be the least surprised, but he could tell that had been a joke. Perhaps sensing his displeasure, the great sage continued:

"Seriously, I doubt it was much different from yourself. I wasn't in any particular rush to acquire the skill, but Kimberly places undue emphasis on combat ability to begin with. Even though there is so much else worth learning."

"...Instructor Gilchrist often makes that argument."

"On that point alone, I agree with her. Despite disagreeing on plenty else."

As they spoke, they were getting higher up. Farquois was not breaking a sweat, but Oliver definitely was—the more he fought gravity, the more it wore him out, and his breath was growing ragged.

"...Ngh..."

"Getting hard for you? Walking is much more difficult than running, yes?"

"...I've been working on slowly improving my time. But that alone... will not get me where you or Instructor Theodore are."

"You plan to match us? Well, the difference in years is not easily overcome, but the goal itself is a fine one. Try jumping," Farquois said, pulling ahead and turning to face him.

This order made Oliver's eyes widen. Jumping while standing on a wall—in his mind, that might as well be throwing yourself off it. They'd left through a third-story window, so they were now very high up.

Eyeing the ground below, Oliver asked, "You want me to fall headfirst?"

"Lord, no. I'm not like your other teachers. I want you to jump and land right where you stand now. Like so."

Farquois demonstrated a few quick hops. An absurd sight—Oliver's head hurt just watching them. Still, he took close observations, analyzing the technique.

The wall was providing no gravitation pull to their feet. If they were returning to the same location, that must have meant some force was filling in for gravity. Arguably, just standing here like this employed the same thing, but with this mage, that force was strong enough to pull them back when contact was severed. In other words...

"...You've strengthened the suction properties... No, you've optimized them."

"See, you're quick on the uptake. It's simply an advanced version of what you're already doing. You're adjusting the handling of your mana to match the general composition of the wall, yes? McFarlane and I carry that to its logical extreme. Always aware of the compositional variation, even the ravages of time, and tweaking the suction property to compensate. That minimizes the fatigue."

Farquois offered a ready explanation, but just imagining how hard that was made Oliver dizzy. Constantly factoring the qualities and condition of the wall, constantly adapting the mana in your feet to match them precisely, and maintaining a false pull between the two— that was the gist of it. Logically sound, but you could find that in the dictionary under the term *armchair theory*.

"Naturally, your five senses won't suffice," said Farquois. "This requires mastery of spatial magic, but you meet that prerequisite. That's why I said this wouldn't take much time. If this was somewhere unknown, it would be another matter—however, you've long since been familiar with Kimberly's walls. You need merely take a closer look. And you will soon realize how slapdash your previous walks have been."

Internally, he was screaming, but here, Oliver's natural obstinance kicked in.

Certainly, he knew how to employ spatial magic to grasp the condition of his footing. There was a delay while his mind processed that, but they were standing still—he only had to focus on a single point. In that light, the order to jump made sense. He was not being given an insurmountable task, and so he buried himself in his spatial senses. Based on that deepened grasp of his footing, he adjusted the mana of his Wall Walk, and his body felt far lighter.

"......!"

"You got it. Now jump."

Farquois gave him no further rope. Feeling like he could now, Oliver kicked right off the wall. He felt the pull on his body from the wall and the ground below, but he strengthened his magical output, prioritizing the artificial pull from the wall. He felt it dragging him back, and both feet landed against it.

"...I did it—?!"

Just as he thought he'd succeeded, his feet slipped—and real gravity got its vengeance. Losing all support, Oliver started to fall, but Farquois had already circled around him and caught him in both arms. As Oliver stared up at the sky, stunned, the great sage smiled.

"You relaxed as your feet made contact, yes? Your landing itself made the wall's properties waver. If you don't compensate for that, this happens."

"...Thanks a lot."

"It was nothing. If you'd fallen, you'd have done something—and I didn't warn you out of sheer whimsy. I did the same thing my first time. If you actually pulled it off, that would have been most vexing."

With that, they set Oliver back on the wall's surface. They shot him a look, demanding another attempt, so he caught his breath and tried again. This time, he made adjustments based on his failure and wavered—but was successful.

Farquois flashed him a grin. "Got it this time. Mm, very good," they said. "Yes, you'll be fine. Doesn't matter how many failures you rack up—you'll all learn to do it. You're *my* students."

An off-the-cuff remark, and it jogged a memory from Oliver's mind. Words his mother said when he'd been little, and marveling at the sight of her standing on air. He sensed the same warmth from this mage; his mind filled with fluster and confusion, and before he knew it, he started to speak.

"Are you—?"

"Mm?"

Farquois turned his way, gentle smile unwavering. Oliver managed to swallow his next words.

He could not ask, *Did you know Chloe Halford?* For that subject to come out of nowhere would be far too incautious—and it terrified him that he'd gotten that close to letting his guard down. Was this mage's charm responsible?

"...No, never mind," Oliver said.

"Oh? Then let's head back. Try to get used to the sensation on the way."

Farquois seemed unbothered by it and turned to go. Oliver followed without another word, unable to decide what he should make of what he'd felt there.

His conversation with Farquois echoing in his mind, he finished the day's classes, and evening arrived. As planned, he met Katie in the hall. They'd submitted the paperwork the other day, and now they were both stepping into a new field.

"...Welp, today's the day, Katie."

"...Mm."

She nodded, a bit stiff, and Oliver studied her closely. It was their first day as members of the seminar, so it was natural to be stressed— but she seemed a bit more cornered than anything. Wondering if Guy's separation was behind it, Oliver prodded the point.

"Seems like you're feeling kind of down. You're not wearing yourself out, are you? We could go another day..."

"N-no, no need! I am hunky-dory! Thinking about all the new things we can learn has me too worked up for my own good!"

She was waving her arms, insistent. Oliver put a hand to his temple, sighing.

"You're clearly forcing it. You don't need to fake it around me. If you don't want to put it off, let's at least walk slowly and settle down."

He reached out and caught her wandering hand. He gave it a tug, prompting her to walk—and a moment later, she nearly jumped out of her skin.

"...Huh? Hands? W-w-we're gonna hold hands?"

"Yeah, you seemed so unsteady on your feet, I couldn't help myself. Do you object?"

"No! No objections whatsoever! I'm sorry!"

"Then good. But why the apology?"

Baffled by her reaction, he pulled Katie along. She shot him a sideways glance as she fought off the urge to check a mirror and see if her face was flushed.

"...I feel like...you're kinda worn-out, too," she managed.

"Yeah... Physically, no problems, but...kind of a lot's happened. I've sorted it out inside, so no need to worry. At the least, I can act like myself."

There, he broke off. They'd been about to round a corner, and Rita Appleton came around it the other direction.

"...Oh..."

".....

All three stopped. An awkward silence followed. Rita's gaze went to Katie, then Oliver, then their clasped hands. Realizing that, he let go of Katie and broke the silence.

"Hello, Ms. Appleton. You had a rough time of it in the lava tree mold. Any trouble with the penalty President Linton doled out?"

"...No, sorry, I did what I did—don't let it get to you."

"Not at all. I'm sure you've had enough lectures for now, so I'm not about to pile on. And I know you were worried about Guy. On that point, I'm rather grateful."

"…I did nothing to earn that. I just forced my way in at the end and accomplished nothing else."

Rita shifted her gaze awkwardly. She seemed stiffer than usual, which bothered Oliver. He didn't know her as well as Guy did, but they'd been friendly for a while. She usually met them in higher spirits. But that cheer had sunk below the surface. He made to speak, hoping further conversation would dig up the cause, but she bowed before he could.

"I'd better get going. I envy your *wonderful friendship*, Ms. Aalto."

With that remark, Rita slipped past and headed down the hall. Katie hadn't said a word; she watched the younger girl go, stunned. Then she doubled over, clutching her head.

"…Augh…"

"Relax, Katie. That *was* a bit barbed. Guess she's got thoughts of her own on Guy."

He figured therein lay the cause. Katie had been thinking along similar lines and was kicking herself.

"I must seem so awful…in her eyes…"

"Because you're with me while Guy's gone? Out of context, I can see how it would look bad, but we've got our reasons. And they're not for anyone else to criticize."

Firm on that point, he held his hand out again. Oliver had let go, imagining how Katie would feel around their junior—but now that Rita was gone, there was no need.

"Come on, Katie," he urged with a smile. "Guy left you in my care. I take pride in that fact, and there's nothing we need to feel guilty about. If I can comfort you in his stead, then that's an honor, and a sign of my respect for him."

Katie gasped, hung her head, then took his hand without looking up. They walked off that way and did not let go until they reached the seminar room.

They announced their arrival and were swiftly escorted to the center of the room. Six other seminar members joined the upperclassman who'd recruited them.

The upperclassman smiled at them across a table covered in documents. "Welcome to our humble seminar," he said. "I didn't expect a decision so soon! Such good news."

With that warm greeting, he began making introductions. Oliver and Katie gave their own names and shook hands with each member in turn. With those pleasantries out of the way, they were led to the document table.

"Ordinarily, we'd love to hold a party and get to know each other, but from what I saw last time, you'd much rather *learn*," the upperclassman said. "We've prepared accordingly. I thought we'd bury your heads in these books—unless you have any objections?"

"N-none! Exactly what I want!" Katie hopped into her seat, thirsty for knowledge, and Oliver settled in next to her. Their uncontained appetite earned them smiles.

"Most promising. Tír creatures themselves are highly dangerous, and credentials and permissions for handling anything in this field are a snarled mess. If you don't have a grasp of those, you can't even reach the start line, but at this stage, nobody wants to waste a bunch of time on technicalities. In other words, we're about to *cram*."

The upperclassman glanced at the other members, and they brought in massive wooden boxes, plopping them down on the table flanking the new arrivals. Wands waved to open the lids; inside were rows of potions. Oliver let out a squeak—this was clearly a test of his mettle.

"Focus potions are on the house. Classic perk of almost any seminar, nothing to get worked up about. Let's get going—if I move too fast for you, just say the word. Until you do, I'm going flat out. If it's any comfort, I haven't slept in three days just to prep this curriculum for you."

That quiet smile spoke volumes.

From then until very late that night, Oliver and Katie would have the term *cram* redefined.

Meanwhile, in another part of the school, Guy was grappling with a new field of his own.

"...Ngh...!"

In a darkened, closed-off interior, he was passing curse energy to the receptacle before him. Curse energy fundamentally preferred animate hosts, but it was possible to magically doctor objects like dolls and trick the energy into believing that receptacle was alive. It did not take long for the curse to corrupt and disintegrate such receptacles, so they could not be used to store the energy, but for wrangling exercise, they sufficed. Working with living things was a closer match to practical applications—but improving his craft did not seem like a fair trade for the consequences of that. It was an approach ill-suited for Guy's character.

The assignment complete, he paused and turned around.

"...How's that? Switched up the conduit and channel. Like you said."

"...Hmm..." Eyes on the crumbling receptacles behind him, the substitute curse instructor, Zelma, folded her arms. "...Exceptional. You sailed past nearly each place I imagined you'd stumble. You should know the work you've completed this week is a training regime that would take the average budding wrangler an entire month. I've had my share of promising students, but few as good as you."

"Don't blow too much air up my ass. I don't need it going to my head."

He shrugged it off, exasperated. Zelma rather enjoyed his discomfort.

"Keeping yourself in check is hardly a bad thing. But clearly, you're still highly resistant to the idea of being a wrangler. Not enjoying living with that in you?"

"Find me anyone who does. I'm here learning because I know this can be a powerful weapon—nothing more, nothing less. Maybe I oughtta ask: Is it good for anything else?"

A blunt question, and Zelma laughed out loud.

"You sure don't hold back. You're one of those boys who back off the more enthusiastically you're invited?"

"I dunno. But Instructor David just said to 'think carefully.'"

"How like him. To me, however, that's a bit too hands-off. I'm more inclined to guide a troubled student."

She moved to the back of the desk, facing Guy across it. Zelma put both arms down, leaning toward him. Each gesture and movement beguiling, which was exactly why Guy could not let himself fully trust her, nor did he try to curry her favor. Like Baldia, she was undoubtedly cursed.

"It's true that curse energy, by its nature, corrupts life. But this is exactly why our world requires wranglers. What would we do without anyone who can manage something that dangerous? I'd argue our contributions to the public good are far more obvious than your average mage. Just living with these curses benefits the world of man—you could think of it in those terms."

Zelma closed her eyes, keeping her tone unruffled. She spoke obvious truths about the nature of curse energy—but Guy did find it rather novel hearing this from the mouth of a wrangler. In hindsight, Baldia had nearly never addressed that side of things. She'd been more inclined to treat herself as the embodiment of loathing and despair, sparing no words to who might be saved by her nature. Guy frowned, considering this. In light of what he'd just heard, Baldia's behavior was rather pitiable.

"In those terms, we can very much call Baldia the savior of our world. If all the curses she harbors were still out there, how many more would have fallen victim to them? As warped as my junior is, I have no end of respect for her. What she carries has only warped her insides—she has retained a human shape. And that is a veritable feat."

"......"

A weighty silence. Sensing her words had resonated with him, Zelma flashed a cheery smile.

"You're impressionable. This speech alone seems to have changed your perspective on wranglers! Consider it the price for my personal instruction. Like Instructor David, I will respect your ultimate decision. The only thing you need to do is avoid letting me tempt you," she told Guy. "That's it for today's lesson—come back in three days' time. I shall tempt you all the more."

With that, she released her student. Guy bowed his head, turned, and left the realm of the curse wrangler, certain he'd be there again.

Even when Guy was back in the hall, Zelma's speech continued spinning in his head. He knew that's exactly what she wanted, but he couldn't stop himself. Every aspect of a wrangler's behavior had meaning—and he was learning that just by example.

"...Can't let my guard down," he muttered, scratching his head. "Damn, every last wrangler is—"

At this point, hands clapped down on both shoulders.

"Huh?"

"We've been waiting for you, Guy!"

"Join us for tea. And don't refuse."

It was the Barthé twins, sporting identically wicked grins. As Guy blinked, a third student trudged up behind them, an exhausted, derisive smile on her lips.

"You heard 'em. Come along. I've already thrown in the towel," Mackley said.

*   *   *

The twins led them down the hall, through a door, and outside the school building. Guy blinked at this and asked the same question he'd been voicing over and over.

"Outside? What kinda tea party is this?"

"You'll find out," Lélia told him. "See, they're in sight."

Her eyes were on the gardens up ahead. A red cloth was laid out on the grass, and the invited guests were sitting directly on it. At the far end was a friend of Guy's—dressed in a Yamatsu kimono, boiling water in an iron kettle. She looked up with a smile.

"Oh, Guy! You've availed us of your presence?"

"Nanao...?! You're in on this? What's going on?"

He blinked, and his gaze shifted to the girl seated opposite Nanao. The girl's back was to him, and her head alone turned, shooting him a grumpy side-eye. There were very few students in his year quite as consistently hostile as this one. The combat league finales had certainly ensured he'd remember her face forever.

"Valois?!"

"...What? Am I not allowed to be here?"

The pure Koutz practitioner Ursule Valois, already bracing for a fight. Guy just blinked at her, and the Barthés offered supplemental information.

"It's an Azian-style tea party. A nice change of pace, yes?"

"She's been inviting Lady Ursule from time to time, and we're tagging along. Since Hibiya's the host, we can rope you in without triggering Reston."

"...You sure are tenacious. I mean, I'm in, but..."

Caught up with their scheme, Guy settled down. Sitting on a cloth without chairs made it seem less like a tea party and more like a mid-hike picnic, but he'd always been the outdoorsy type and felt right at home. Sweet treats on a pottery plate were deposited before him; it seemed Nanao was personally preparing each cup of tea. Figuring that would be worth waiting for, he turned his gaze from Lélia to Gui to Mackley.

"Guess I'd better say sorry. A friend of mine went off on you a bit—my bad. I went down first thing, didn't manage to stop him."

"Don't worry about it. We were careless," Lélia replied. "We bear no grudge against Reston. It's entirely true that, out of context, what we said sounded like we were trying to pry you away."

"Easy for you to say. His damn golem stabbed me in the back of the neck!" Mackley griped.

"Let it go," said Gui. "We healed you up. And that could easily have been me or my sister. You just had the bad luck to be standing against the wall."

"Show me one person who'd be convinced by *that* argument!" Mackley fumed, her cry echoing across the blue sky, loud enough that Nanao and Valois heard her.

"I can't settle down with you yelliiing? The wind keeps bringing in bits of grass. Whyyy can't we do this inside?"

"We certainly could, but a change of scene will do us wonders. There are pleasures in a boisterous assembly as well as a quiet one."

As she answered, Nanao busied herself with the tea, putting leaves in a prewarmed cup, adding water heated to the ideal temperature, and stirring it with a kind of dampened whisk.

Valois took a seat, watching this process unfold. Despite her barbed words, she was sitting bolt upright on her knees—not a posture present in Union culture, so this showed she'd arrived with prior knowledge. Grateful for that, Nanao put the thought into words.

"Your *seiza* is elegant and beautiful. I appreciate the effort to match the occasion. But pray, relax and enjoy yourself. Tea can be a ceremonial occasion, but I barely remember the manners myself. I will spare not one word to what is proper, and you need not concern yourself with errors."

This just served to deepen Valois's frown. Her grandmother had drilled the importance of etiquette into her from an early age;

attempting to emulate the formalities of the occasion was now unconscious, instinctive. Yet, this girl claimed that was of no importance—and that left Valois unsure how to comport herself.

Nanao finished the tea and placed it softly before Valois.

"Enjoy. Do not let the involved process stay your tongue. If you like it, splendid; if you do not, so be it. Give me your unvarnished opinion."

Valois gingerly lifted the cup with both hands. It was perhaps a third full of a frothing green liquid. Remembering the manners she'd read about beforehand, she made to turn the cup three times but soon realized Nanao had no interest in such formalities. For that reason, she moved it directly to her lips. The foreign flavors spread across her tongue, and she slowly drank.

After allowing herself some time to process it, she spoke.

"...It's very...bitter...? Buuut it goes down easier than I thought. Does adding air to it aid with the mouthfeel? I suppooose that would serve the same function as our milk?"

"Ah, you picked up on that? I was quite surprised by the local custom of adding cow's milk to tea. Once I adjusted to that, I realized the similarities. Perhaps adding milk is even more expedient."

Nanao was preparing cups for the other guests as she spoke. The process seemed far too inefficient given each was the same—it would have been much quicker if she had used a spell or prepared some magic tool. But Nanao deliberately brewed one cup at a time, carrying each to their seats on her own two feet. When everyone was served, she returned to Valois, facing her once more.

"Yet, I believe there is meaning in these procedures, too. I see you have noticed that yourself."

"...Weeell, I guess? If I watch you painstakingly make it, I am naturally inclined to savor the taaaste... These are tea sweets?"

"Indeed. You may slice them with a pick or grasp them in your hands—eat however you wish."

Valois reached for the little treat on the tray. Theodore had brought some red beans back for Nanao, which she had used to make her own paste for *kintsuba*. Valois prodded her *kintsuba* with the pick and found it soft and yielding; she sliced a quarter off it, poked it with the pick, and carried it to her mouth.

It had a richer sweetness than she'd expected; it was almost too much for her, but then she blinked and took another sip of tea. The bitterness of the beverage balanced out the sweetness lingering on her tongue—and felt like a revelation. This was a flavor experience that required both tea and sweets to be complete.

"…Mind if I move off my feet?" she asked properly.

"By all means. You may lay down on your back if you see fit," Nanao replied serenely.

Valois shifted her weight off her lower legs, relaxing on the cloth, her eyes drifting to the clear skies above. While her mind was preoccupied with ritual, she hadn't noticed how freeing that sight was—and before she knew it, she was speaking to that.

"…Is thiiis what you meant…?" Valois wondered.

"Oh, is that an epiphany?"

"…Loosely, yes? I thiiink I see the concept of your tea party. The tension's draining from my shoulders… I don't care about the fuss over there anymore. Even this wind…at this time of year, it's just pleasant. Aaand…the sunlight and grass…the smell of the soil…"

She closed her eyes, soaking it in.

Once, she'd been confined to a basement room. Cornered while she went half mad, swearing to take her little friend out of there—a goal that was not meant to be. That had stolen a piece of her heart away, but now even that gap felt comfortable.

Nanao finished preparing her own tea last and sat sipping on it, gazing at Valois's face. She'd caught glimpses of Valois's history on that blood-soaked stage, and now as Valois relaxed, defenseless, Nanao perceived it once again.

"There is sadness in your eyes. I thought as much. I ventured you would prefer this to the confines of a tearoom," said Nanao. "…I feel as if I have been away from this too long. Below the heavens, my own feet upon the ground—a fundamental delight allowed to all those who live."

As Valois's heart thawed, her painful past came into view. Her gaze left the sky, dancing back to Nanao's face—and a tear ran down her cheek.

"Covell."

Nanao smoothly drew her wand, drawing a blackout veil between Valois and the other guests. A gesture of kindness—and Valois wiped the tumbling tears with her sleeve, her voice trembling.

"...Howww could you tell?" she asked.

"We have fought in earnest once. You may shed as many tears as you see fit. I imagine you have been storing them for quite a while."

Nanao dropped her gaze to her tea, taking a sip.

Across the veil, all that could be seen of their exchange was a hazy silhouette. But the glimpse they'd caught before it was drawn had been enough for both Barthés to glean their mistress's state.

"...Can't believe it," Gui muttered. "Did you see—?"

"Keep your voice down, fool," Lélia hissed. "Do not disturb them with needless commotion. This a vital moment for Lady Ursule."

She looked grateful—but also repentant.

"Would that Hibiya mentor me? Our minds are linked directly, yet she is closer to Lady Ursule's heart than we have ever been. No, perhaps it's the other way around. Why can we not do the same? That is our shame."

"Don't overthink it," Guy said, munching on a *kintsuba* in his bare hand. "I've seen with my own eyes how unique she is. Ain't something you can just imitate. You'll just have to slowly work on getting closer. Not by force like that link between minds—just the way everyone else does."

He took a gulp of tea to wash the sweet down and turned to face the twins.

"I ain't one to reap all the benefits, so lemme give some advice. You two spending any time with Valois? Since you got back to campus, you seem...stabler..."

Aware of the delicate situation, he prodded that issue carefully. But Lélia caught the nuance beneath his words. Her cheeks stiffened, and she gave her brother a look.

"Gui..."

"Sorry, I told him. I was pretty, uh, far gone at the time."

Lélia buried her face in her hands.

"Huh? What're we talking about?" Mackley asked, lost.

Not about to explain the whole thing over again, Lélia paid her no attention.

"...Much as I'd love to dig a hole and crawl into it," she managed, "I guess we're past carrying about appearances. And Guy—we owe you a lot, so if you're offering, I'll swallow my shame and take you up on it. You're right, we're better. Lady Ursule's not distancing herself from us anymore. She's making a point of keeping us around. And we're grateful for it."

"If you choke up there, we won't get anywhere, Lélia. What we gotta talk about is what's next," Gui said, one hand on his sister's quivering shoulders.

"Uh, don't overthink things, either," Guy added. "If going with the flow takes you places, that's totally fine. Just... I got thoughts on what you shared before. Like—I got options, and you kinda don't."

"Seriously, someone clue me in," said Mackley.

"Yeah, but that's a servant's lot in life. Might be hard for you to wrap your head around, but from the moment we were born, we were meant to serve her. When that relationship was on the rocks, it was a living hell, but thanks to you, we're back to normal—and frankly, far better than before. I'm not about to call that good enough, but for now—no need to worry. And I got my dumbass little brother with me."

"Yep, yep, with you to the end, O wise sister. See? She's kinda cute when she's down, but the second she perks up, she's gotta lord it over everyone. Even though we're twins and the age difference is negligible."

"That negligible difference set our fates in stone. Wallow in regret, Little Brother. Repent being too lazy to race me out the womb."

The more they talked, the more Lélia got her groove back; she and her brother were trading barbs. Guy was relieved to see it, but Mackley just smiled brightly and drew her wand.

"...Frag–"

"Don't, Mackley! Sorry we left you hanging! Put the wand away!"

"Hear me out! I'll ignore whoever I want, but if you ignore me— well, I'd rather be surrounded by slugs. Try it again, and I'll blow you all up and fuck off home."

Mackley was so pissed, her voice had gone *flat*, and everyone rushed to placate her.

Sensing the commotion across the blackout veil, Valois was still shedding tears; Nanao was preparing a second cup of tea for her. By the time she finished it, she'd likely work things out. The sky above would never change, and even now, she was still free to run about the land beneath it.

"Mm, a fine day," Nanao whispered, satisfied.

She stayed seated beside a wounded heart, offering comfort as the tea party continued on.

Six hours of ultra-compressed leaning at the very limit of their processing power, and it struck Oliver that going further without pausing to collect themselves would be actively harmful. He voiced that concern, and the upperclassman teaching them accepted it with a grin— and stood up, only to swoon and collapse. Only half awake, he was carried out by the other seminar members. The preparation fatigue had clearly caught up with him.

"...Transport requires supervision by four or more mages, including the one granted express permission. Am I right, Katie?" Oliver asked.

"...Wait, there might be another restriction. There was an example..."

Oliver and Katie were left behind, with only one older member to keep an eye on them.

For a long time, they busied themselves reviewing what they'd been taught, making sure it was all steeped into their heads. Oliver was keen on the daily acquisition of new knowledge, but it had been a long time since he tried to force quite this much in at once. Alone, he'd have suffered, but with Katie at his side, it went down easy. He'd always admired her passion for her studies, and the desire to keep up gave him boundless energy. The empty focus potion bottles continued to mount.

Ultimately, they hit the time limit before their concentration petered out. The corner of his eye saw the clock at midnight, and he closed the file with a *thump*.

"...It's awfully late. Katie, let's call it a day. The others are waiting for us at the base."

"...Oh, is it that time?" she asked, looking up. "It is! I've gotta prep for tomorrow..."

She vaulted from her seat and started putting the documents away. Oliver helped her get it done quickly. They bowed their heads to the upperclassman on monitoring duty and left the seminar room. They'd agreed to spend the night in their workshop, not the dorms—and so they raced down the corridors, the threat of encroachment present but no longer posing any danger.

"The moment the lecture began, you got your stride back. Nobody focuses like you. It was all I could do to keep up."

"Th-that's hardly true. I just keep racing on ahead, heedless, and you forcing us to turn back and take in the big picture really helped."

"Oh? Then maybe we're a good match as research partners. Maybe that's why he said we had synergy."

He hadn't paid that comment much attention in their first visit but was nodding at it now. Katie watched his profile, feeling emotions welling up inside. As they lined up by the painting to the labyrinth, her lips parted.

"...Um..."

"Mm?"

"...Maybe a bit late for this, but I'm really glad you joined the seminar with me. If it was just me today...I bet I'd have been there till dawn."

She knew just what she'd been like during the cram session. She knew that was a bad habit but had never been able to stop herself. Once she got her head buried in something, both pain and time disappeared. Pete had similar propensities, but he was nowhere near as bad as Katie got on certain subjects. More than once, a magical beast had torn her arm off, and all she'd done was stop the bleeding and go right back to making observations.

"And the whole time I was reading tír documents, I felt secure. When I'm studying on my own, I get lost in it, but with someone I can trust, like you or Guy, I know you'll pull me back. S-sorry, that's so weirdly dependent. I shouldn't—"

Shame got the better of her, and she tried to walk it back, but Oliver shook his head, looking deeply relieved.

"There's nothing strange about it. I'm glad I can play that role for you. Yeah, that works. While Guy's gone, let me be your anchor."

He smiled at her, like this thought filled him with joy. And when she saw that—the emotions swelling up inside Katie shot way over a threshold, trying to race off without her consent. Barely keeping them in check, she yelped his name.

"...Oliver!"

This was quite loud. He looked surprised, and she squeaked the next words out. As if she could barely stand to wait for them.

"...C-can I get...a hug?"

"...? Uh, sure..."

A modest request, and he spread his arms. As he did, Katie pulled him into an embrace. Feeling his warmth against the length of her.

His scent, his weight. Something that hovered right there at her side, but with which she dared not make contact. Only allowing herself to accept the occasional overflow, desperately waiting for it like a desert waited for rain.

"...I'm sorry... I'm sorry..."

"What for? We've had this free-hug policy for ages. If anything, you've held off on it for too long."

He mussed up her hair as he spoke. Ordinarily, Oliver didn't do this to her, even when they were hugging. A habit of his that Guy had unsuccessfully warned him of—but he knew Katie had always rather liked it. Now that he was filling in for Guy, he gave himself free reign.

"____"

And in this moment alone, that unfettered expression of affection melted Katie's restraints with terrifying ease. Appalling thoughts flooded her mind.

He would probably agree to anything she asked of him. An act akin to helping yourself to water from a well dug by your neighbor, diving into the communal spring waters with dirty boots on and scooping handfuls to your lips. But the boy before her would likely allow it all.

"...Haah! ...Haah..."

"...You okay there, Katie? Your breathing's kinda..."

Maddening—this impulse, this thirst. To her disgust, she was barely holding herself a half step away from acting upon it. Adoration, longing, and carnal desire melded into a single need, haloed by the inherently dicey instincts of a *mage*. A rejected part of her mind was screaming at her: *Don't you dare let him go. No matter the consequences, you must make him yours. You can't let him get away. This is something you cannot live without.*

It would get the best of her. That warning bell rang before her rationality slipped away, and Katie bit down hard on the flesh of her cheek.

Pain and blood followed, a harsh cure that woke her sanity up—this was little different from what Valois had done in the combat league.

But it worked. While the pain distracted her, she freed herself from the embrace, prying her body from the warmth that tempted her heart astray.

She knew better than to let the blood escape her lips. She swallowed it all—and did her very best to plaster on a smile.

"…Thanks. I'm okay now," Katie said. "Let's go! They're waiting for us at the base!"

With that, Katie spun around and leaped into the painting. Sensing something highly unstable in her act, Oliver followed, spurred by his own anxieties.

Once in the labyrinth, things were blessedly uneventful; they followed the shortest route to their workshop. Nanao, Pete, and Chela were already there; Oliver and Katie had lingered in that seminar far too long. As they stepped in, Chela gave them a warm smile.

"Welcome home! We're all here at last."

Oliver knew she'd stopped herself from adding *except for Guy.* She turned and started prepping tea, appearing for all the world as if she cared only about easing their fatigue.

"You've had a lot on your plates," she told Oliver and Katie. "Once you're ready for tomorrow, sit down and relax a moment. Of course, if you wish to go straight to bed, don't let me stop you. Your beds are made and ready for you."

"Oh, thanks, Chela. We'll take you up on that." Oliver smiled back, then glanced at Katie.

She'd babbled the whole time they were in the labyrinth, not letting him get a word in edgewise, but she'd clammed up the moment they'd stepped into the base. Something was clearly off. She was standing perfectly still just inside the door, eyes unfocused and aimed at empty space.

"Hrm—"

"Hey, what's wrong?"

Nanao and Pete soon spotted it and put down their work. Chela broke away from her tea prep, swiftly running to Katie's side.

"Katie? Are you okay? You don't seem…"

"…Huh? N-no, I'm fine…"

She shook her head slowly, clearly unaware of her own condition.

Chela grabbed her hand. "I find that hard to believe. Let me have a look at you. This way."

She pulled her into the back room. Katie didn't resist, and the others watched them go with concern.

Chela sat Katie down on a bed and made to give her a thorough exam. The curly-haired girl's answer a moment ago had felt off, so Chela started there.

"You have a cut inside your mouth? Open wide—let me see."

Katie dithered a moment but soon opened her mouth. Chela was not surprised to see a lengthy cut on the right cheek. Natural mage healing had stopped the bleeding, but the cause of the wound was all too obvious.

"You…bit yourself?" Chela asked, frowning. "And rather forcefully. Why would you…?"

As she spoke, she drew her wand, healing the wound. This took no time at all, but Katie's gaze remained unfocused, her condition unimproved. Surmising the root cause lay elsewhere, Chela looked the rest of her over.

"…Hmm. Your mana circulation's a tad rapid and uneven. Your heart's beating fast, your eyes dilated. But why, I wonder? These seem less like symptoms and more like a state of excitement that refuses to go away."

Voicing her best diagnosis, Chela crooked her head. Katie appeared to be only half listening.

"Any clue why?" Chela asked. "Did you drink any potions?"

"...Potions? Oh... We downed a lot of focus potions at the seminar... Maybe that's why..."

"At your seminar? Oh, I see. Upperclassmen likely brew them strong, reformulating them for extra effectiveness. If you went through a lot, I'd see why that would unsettle your physique. Still..."

That seemed a likely cause but did not fully explain her condition. Chela's friends had suffered adverse effects from standard-issue potions before, but she had no memories of symptoms presenting like this. It was always possible an upperclassman had simply provided really potent potions, but in that case, Oliver should be suffering similarly. Leaving antidotes and bloodletting off the table for now, Chela probed further.

"...You seem to be suffering more than that. Your physical symptoms aren't that strong, so I have to assume your mentality is a factor. Was there some strong stimulus? Something that rocked your emotions one way or the other?"

She had a hunch this was primarily emotional—and Katie visibly flinched. It took her a long time to speak.

"...Well...I've been with Oliver all this time...and...near the end... we hugged..."

"...Oh."

Chela closed her eyes, nodding as the last piece fell into place.

Excessive focus potion intake had been merely the foundation. Close contact with Oliver in that condition had proved a trigger, putting her nervous system in a state of excitement that refused to subside. All spurred on by her recent mental instability and the brakes coming off her self-control. In other words, excitement and exhaustion had left her dazed and confused. With that diagnosis reached, Chela gave her a hug.

"Understood. I'm sorry for prying," Chela offered. "But if we don't do anything, you won't be able to sleep tonight. And you've got an early morning tomorrow, right? If we use spells or potions to force you asleep, that'll take its toll on you..."

Knowing the cause led to other concerns. Katie's nerves were already so wound up. Antidotes or bloodletting would not have much effect. Knocking her out with a spell—she might as well just faint, meaning that was out of the question. So what would be effective against the symptoms?

Chela ran through her options and latched on to one.

"...Hmm..."

Not bad on the face of it. Arguably the ideal solution. It would help Katie recover and help Chela advance things toward her own goal—two birds with one stone. Convinced of that, Chela moved to put it into action. She let go of Katie, stood up, and spoke, keeping her voice ever so pleasant.

"I have an idea. Can you wait here a minute, Katie?"

"......?"

Katie managed a vague nod and watched Chela leave. Clueless as to what her friend's idea might be or what it would involve.

The door opened softly, and Chela stepped out. All eyes converged on her.

"Well, Chela? How is she?" Oliver asked.

"Oliver, Nanao, join me a moment?"

She beckoned them toward the door to the other bedroom. This was the men's side, used for sleeping and changing. Oliver and Nanao exchanged a glance, then went in ahead of her.

Chela shot Pete a meaningful look; catching her drift, he returned a slight nod. With that, Chela closed the door behind her, took a breath, and faced her friends.

"First, Katie's condition. She was emotionally unstable to begin with, then overindulged in focus potions—she's temporarily in a state of nervous excitement. That itself is no real concern. Her body will naturally restore itself if we wait—but she won't be able to sleep tonight."

The results of her examination left Oliver looking grim. Mages were accustomed to using focus potions when cramming, but he'd been aware of Katie's condition—he should have stopped her from consuming that many. Sensing his regrets, Chela kept calm.

"With lingering fatigue, her recovery will be slow, and if she uses more potions to compensate for that, it could compound the issue. For that reason, I'd like to free her from the state and let her rest. Are we in agreement there?"

"Mm, naturally," said Nanao.

"Oh yeah, of course, but..."

Oliver was slightly more hesitant than Nanao. He could tell this was leading up to something—which meant it was a proposition that would be difficult to accept without the preamble. Keeping a close eye on Oliver's reactions, Chela proceeded with caution.

"That would be your healing, Oliver. There's no better means of easing her excited nerves without burdening her physically. But I'm concerned that ordinary approaches would have little effect on a condition this extreme. I'd recommend a stronger tactic."

Her loaded phrasing made a chill run down his spine. He hoped he was reading too much into it. He desperately hoped she did not mean what he thought she did.

Praying internally that he had leaped to a foolish conclusion, he had to ask, "...And...what do you mean by that, Chela?"

"Ideally, you will bring her to climax. If you'll allow me to be blunt."

Exactly the answer he'd feared, and it hit him like a brick. Nanao blinked, not immediately catching on. Reeling, Oliver took several steps sideways.

"...You want me...to get her off?"

"That is why I called Nanao in as well. Even I realize this will require you both to agree. What do you say, Nanao? Let me know your honest thoughts on Oliver handling Katie that way."

By this point, Nanao had worked out what Chela was proposing. A privilege only she had enjoyed—would she allow Katie to join in on it? She got exactly why this question came to her. Oliver was staring at her profile, hoping she would protest—but she hesitated a long moment, then smiled.

"By all means. How could I object? If this is what Katie requires..."

"——!"

Oliver's heart leaped to his throat. He was well aware one path to escape had been cut off.

"Understood," Chela said, nodding. She turned to face him. "We have Nanao's permission. The choice is yours, Oliver."

He could not run from this question. His extremities went numb, and his throat was instantly parched, like he was breathing hot air. His mind was sluggish, but he forced it to form words.

"...Listen, Chela," he faltered. "Guy...left Katie in my hands..."

"I am aware. That is why maintaining her condition falls to you. Am I out of line?"

"...You are not, in principle. Just—there are means we should avail ourselves of and means we should not. So that I may hold my head high and return her to Guy when he comes back. And you're acting in full knowledge of that, right?"

His voice broke, unable to bottle up his emotions. Anger on his face, lashing back to a degree far beyond mere reluctance. Chela met this head-on, unwavering.

"Naturally. And in light of that, I believe this is a means we *should* take. And an act that *is* permitted within our ranks," she said. "Take a step back from that. Why do you think Guy has been dutifully taking care of Katie all this time? Because he's her friend and he loves her? That's a given. But, Oliver, it was also meant to reduce the burden on *you*. So that Katie did not ask too much of you, to keep her from becoming unbalanced—he's taken on that role this whole time, asking for no help from anyone."

That was a gut punch. He knew all too well he could not refute it. Guy maintained his easygoing act but was always trying to help Oliver out, shouldering anything he possibly could. And inarguably, the biggest baggage he'd picked up was Katie. This should have fallen to Oliver. He'd admired the way she chose to come to Kimberly with views that were a minority here—and he'd been the first to push her along that path. But with large chunks of his attention diverted to Nanao and Pete, he lacked the capacity to properly look after her from close at hand. Guy had taken care of her for him all this time. No one had asked him to; he'd simply decided that was his role.

"If I could shoulder that burden, I would have long ago," Chela added. "This is not because Katie and I are the same gender—rather, I am simply not you or Guy. Even within the Sword Roses, only the two of you have forged a relationship where this treatment would be possible. And with one option gone, only you can fill in. I trust you see the logic in this."

Mercilessly making sense, she was pinning him down. And he knew this had been a chess gambit designed to corner him. She'd come in with a path to checkmate—and unless she made a false move, the outcome would not change. Naturally, she was laying the foundation to that end.

"And I'll add this is not just tonight. Katie will remain unstable until Guy returns, and it's highly possible she'll need similar handling. Debating the merits of it each time would be fruitless—let us chart our course here, tonight. If we do this now, we will continue to do so. If we reject the idea, then we will not entertain it again. Which decision will you make, Oliver?"

That question was checkmate. She'd said everything she had to say and made the final choice his—objectively a *fair* approach. But Chela herself knew the reality was quite the opposite. Oliver could not say no here. He was not the kind of man who could let a friend suffer simply because he did not *want* to.

This lay deeper inside him than his own self-loathing, the nature that drove Oliver Horn. Chela did not know the specifics of what lay beneath that, but she knew what type of man her friend was. So she'd brought up his obligations to Guy, filled in the moat around Castle

Oliver. She did not need to collapse the keep itself. He'd never had a resistance marshaled there.

With all arguments taken from him, Oliver stood in silence. Nanao put her arms around his shoulders.

"Oliver, let me join you," she whispered.

"...Nana...o...?"

"I shall accompany you both. 'Tis an extension of what we've done so many times. My arms around Katie from behind as you hug us both. Thus, Katie will stop herself from asking anything of you."

He gaped at her. Naturally, Nanao knew exactly what was going through his mind. But she was equally aware of how much Katie was suffering. Her friend's desire had long been thwarted—and Nanao had grown enough in her time here to realize that it was *she* who had robbed Katie of that opportunity.

She did not believe that was justified. A furor yet simmered deep within Nanao's heart. No matter how often their trysts, no matter how much she succumbed to them—to this day, a portion of her wanted nothing more than to lay her life against the one she loved. She was only too conscious of her inhumanity. Thus, she entertained no hopes. And deemed herself unfit to deny a friend her burning need.

It was downright ironic. If either one of them had been in their right mind, they'd have dismissed the proposition out of hand. But right here and now, in a merciless twist of fate, two warped souls each accepted Chela's suggestion. Thus, it was checkmate. The ploy dreamed up by Chela—the witch named Michela McFarlane—proved a success.

"I think that's a grand idea," Chela said. "With Nanao nearby, expressing approval, Katie's reluctance to accept treatment will fade away. If you're in, we should handle this quickly. The longer we stand here, the less time Katie has to sleep."

The victorious witch urged action, using logic as a shield. Already out of words to fight her, with Nanao's eyes boring into him, Oliver listlessly nodded. Together, they set out. But as they left the room, he directed one last barb back at his friend.

"...Is this really the right choice, Chela?"

"Undoubtedly. I swear it upon my name."

Her smile was free of any shadows. Much like Miligan's when they first met.

The face of a true mage, Oliver thought as he shriveled up inside.

Katie had been waiting in the other bedroom, and two friends came to see her. Too dazed to pick up on the grim mood, she simply looked up at them.

"...Mm? Oliver and Nanao? Why are you both...? Where's Chela?"

"...Katie, I know you're in rough shape, but we need to talk."

Oliver knelt down before her. Head down, not meeting her eyes. He was afraid to do so.

"You're upset by Guy's absence, and the focus potions compounded that—your nervous system's all wired up and won't settle down. Given the cause, spells and potions won't be effective, and we've concluded the best solution would be healing arts. If you're open to it, I'll be taking care of that."

It took a while for this explanation to filter down. His words echoed in her mind, and as she worked out what that meant, her pulse began to race. She addressed the top of Oliver's head.

"You...treating me? Um, like...on my back?"

"Focusing there. Avoiding sensitive areas as much as possible. But... no matter where I touch you, the results will be much the same. We'll be quelling your excitement by first raising it to the brink. In other words...bringing you to climax."

Again, it took a while for this to sink in. Climax? To what? Her thoughts were worryingly dull. But she was not young enough to remain clueless forever. The context eventually led to her parsing the meaning behind the phrase. She stiffened up, then burst out laughing.

"…Ah-ha-ha-ha…! Oh, I must be dreaming. I knew something was wrong! You'd never talk about this with *Nanao* here."

"'Tis no dream, Katie. Alas, I have made you suffer greatly."

Nanao sat down on the bed next to her, pulling her close. And catching the fragrance steeped into her uniform, Katie was forced to admit this was really happening. Her smile froze, and her voice shook.

"…Y-you've gotta be kidding. If this isn't a dream, then is it some sort of prank? Th-that's a bit mean, really. Does it end when I agree? Will everyone come out and laugh…?"

"Not a single one of your friends would ever dream of doing anything that cruel to you. I don't mean to rush you—take your time and choose. I'll add that if you wait the night out, this should subside on its own. You likely won't get a wink of sleep, but if you'd rather take that approach, that's fine. I'll stay up with you—to make up for this proposal."

Oliver's voice was tense. However, he would not let himself phrase that option as if he preferred it. He knew that would make her dig in and endure. But the grim tone he took was turning the screws on Katie—only now did she realized that this *would* happen if she wanted it.

"…N-no sleep would be rough, ah-ha-ha. I've got an early morning… J-just…? That doesn't mean…"

"Enough, Katie," Nanao said when Katie tried laughing it off. "You need not hold yourself back."

Nanao tightened her embrace. Seeing Katie like this was sad and painful and made her want to cry. Feeling her heat against her, Nanao thought, *How many trials has she endured for the sake of a friend as inhumane as I?*

"I should have told you long ago—Oliver is not my possession. I never had a right to demand that of him, nor did I ever wish to take him from you. Thus…"

"...Eep...?!"

Nanao had run her fingers down Katie's sides. Not her usual impish jab, but a tender caress, with foreplay as the intent. The stimulus made Katie shiver, and in her ear, Nanao breathed the last words to topple her fortress.

"...Myself included, tonight, we indulge. Should you care to join us."

Too many thoughts and feelings were spinning in Katie's head. This was so far beyond her understanding—and she'd long since run out of rope to restrain herself with. She should stop thinking and give herself over to this. There was nothing here to be afraid of. Just two close friends, thinking of her, loving her, and trying to comfort her. Whatever happened next, she need not worry about the outcome. On that one point, she was very clear.

Yet, another part of her was yelling that this could not be. There were a lot of reasons for that.

All that time you've spent with Guy, and the moment he leaves, you're gonna turn right to Oliver and let him administer to your basest needs? How will you ever face Guy when he comes back after something that shameless? Why are you so unprincipled? Can you not just grin and bear it? Why can you not simply last out the night?

Another part of her whispered, *Well, can you?*

Can you refuse and wait out the night? Laying with Oliver, his touch spurned, Nanao offering you comfort? Wondering the whole night long what it would have been like to feel his hands on you? Or will you insist you can't handle that and hole up in bed alone? The covers pulled over your head, unable to sleep, tormented by those exact same fantasies? Well aware Oliver lies asleep in the room next door? Imagining his sleeping face, his breath, his warmth? Wondering if he'd still touch you if you asked, though you've already chosen not to?

You can't.

You'd never last the night. It'd drive you mad.

"...Ah..."

She had her answer. Not one riding the crest of her endlessly swelling urge, but a conclusion reached by her rational mind, even as the desire threatened to snuff it out. She realized that, from the start, she'd been laboring under a misapprehension. This had never been a choice. She was past that point already. She knew for a fact she *could not refuse.*

She heard Guy's voice. *Don't push yourself.* One hand on his hip, scoffing. Matching pace with her like a brother, with tender care—just like he always did.

Her eyes filled with tears. Was this a vision designed to comfort her, or was it how he really felt? Katie could no longer tell.

"......Please...touch me......"

"...Okay," Oliver acknowledged with a metallic tone.

He drew his wand and cast a sound dampening spell on the door. Nanao slipped around behind Katie, not letting go of her. Oliver glanced at Katie—and began moving like a precision machine.

He knew just what to do. His hands knew all too well how to take care of this.

"I get why you thought that was the time, but actually putting that in action?" Pete said.

He and Chela were waiting in the living room while Katie's treatment was underway. Pete sounded like he'd heard every word the trio had spoken, and Chela frowned at him. Then she saw the cicada-sized golem resting on his fingertip.

"...Will you stop that?" she said with a sigh. "Listening in on your friends' conversations with golems! You knew I'd relay the contents to you afterward."

"I could've waited but was a little worried—and I was right to be."

He turned a page in the book he was reading. Chela pulled her wand and put a sound dampening spell on the door just in case, then moved over near him, arms folded.

"And what was wrong with it? My core stance is exactly like yours,

Pete. Increase the bonds among the Sword Roses any way we can, make them as strong as possible, until our group cannot be broken. This moment was ripe to do just that, so I acted on it." She put a hand to her chest, smiling. "Oliver and Nanao's bond, Guy and Katie's— each glad tidings. But two pairs in isolation is hardly enough. That alone still carries the threat of Oliver and Nanao fighting to the death, or Guy and Katie getting consumed by the spell together. That is why we need further chains connecting them laterally. Having multiple partners presents no issues here."

Chela was quite firm on that. The idealization of monogamy was for *ordinaries*. Mages did not see things that way, and the Sword Roses need not be bound to it. Pete had long been in agreement there and nodded.

"I'm acting on that idea myself. Just be ready for the consequences," he cautioned.

"...Namely?"

"You don't know, huh? I thought as much. When you've got tunnel vision, you lose track of where the line is. Way worse than I do. Given your background, I imagined you would."

He sighed and closed the book, putting it down. Then he stood up and faced Chela, looking right into her eyes, like he was persuading a child.

"Listen close. You talked Oliver into this not as a friend, but as a mage. You spun a web of logic and bent his will. That process is a bigger problem than the outcome. I did the same thing myself, so I'm not one to talk."

Pete made a face, remembering his blunder. Chela shifted her gaze, at least somewhat aware.

"...If I didn't, Oliver and Katie would never get any closer," she countered. "They've been drawn to each other all this time, but neither one will let themselves act on the attraction. If we don't push them across that line..."

"I know. Free hugs alone didn't do the trick. Sounds like poly relationships are pretty common in mage circles, and boosting our physical intimacy sets the stage—or so you thought, but that proved optimistic, right?"

Her past actions revealed her motives.

"But it was partially effective!" Chela insisted. "Routine hugs normalized healing one another, and that lowered the hurdle to what they're doing now. Without that foundation, the argument I just made would never have worked. I could push them here because we were already at the stage where this was normal—I only acted because I decided they were ready. I'm not rushing things!"

"I get where you're coming from. But Oliver's a tough customer. He's got his own hang-ups."

Pete shrugged, perfectly aware he'd not picked up on those until it was too late—so why would she? All he could do was prepare her for it. And when things did not go the way she expected, he would help her through it.

"You've blown past those this time. That's why there'll be consequences. You'll soon see if I'm worried about nothing."

With that, he sat back down and resumed his reading. It still didn't make sense to Chela, but she took a seat herself, sipping her now-cold tea.

"...Hyaaaaa...!"

Katie let out a yelp. Nothing had even happened yet; Oliver's fingers had just barely touched her sides.

That alone provoked a marked change in her current state. Like a balloon inflated to the bursting point, Oliver thought. This treatment would require delicacy. Even with his technical expertise, it would be no small task to let the air out without having her burst.

"...Mm...! Ah... Haah... Wahlih...!"

He began by lightly brushing her skin through her shirt. Getting her used to the sensation, then letting trace amounts of mana flow—intentionally in less effective locations. His hands went around her narrow waist, from her sides to her back, gradually expanding the range of his caresses. Nothing on the front yet. He was taking great care not to burden her weary body, just gently, easily stacking on the layers of pleasure.

"…How sweet, Katie. To hear you moan like this…"

"…Don't…whisper in my ear, Nanao…! You're driving me nuts…"

Nanao was backing Oliver from a different vector. They were in sync, even now, and Oliver had no idea how he was meant to feel about *that*. He chose not to think about it, focusing on the movement of his hands. He could drown in self-recriminations later—right now, he had to heal his friend. If this ended without achieving that goal, then he'd be useless. Calling him a filthy animal would far too mild.

"…Are you…crying, Oliver…?" Katie asked.

The last words he'd expected. It took a moment for him to even absorb what she'd said, then he felt a drop land on his arm—and realized tears were falling. His self-loathing threatened to overwhelm him.

What gives you the right to such tears? Or are these drops composed of the same stuff that goes in a golem? Axle grease or antifreeze? Perhaps you've truly broken down, a hole yawning open in your exoskeleton.

"Don't mind me. I'm going a bit…nuts myself."

He moved to the next stage of treatment. Trusting he need no longer keep her clothing in the way, he undid the buttons on her shirt and slid his hands inside.

This is nothing new. When was I last sane? That ended the night I harbored my mother's soul. The path I've followed since is as twisted as my heart's become—maybe this outcome was inevitable. Like with my mother, this moment is a turning point. The last night that I can be purely a good friend to Katie or Guy.

"…Ah… AH…… Aughhh…!"

Having built a stimulus foundation on her sides and back, he now moved his hands to the untouched frontiers in front. A finger slid beneath her skirt, down her lower abdomen, and tracing the top of her shorts. He need not invade those. However, from here on out, it was all erogenous zones. His right fingers pressed against her womb, injecting mana hard, while his left fingertip spun within her navel.

"……~~~~~~~~!!!!!!!!"

The dams burst, and a wave of pleasure coursed through Katie like an electric current. A single orgasm was not the end—leaving gaps timed to the second, he repeatedly stimulated both womb and navel. A chain of crests built upon a careful foundation.

As her body bucked, Nanao gently cradled her. Katie was tensed up for the better part of a minute before it all drained away. Feeling certain he'd brought her to a flawless finish, Oliver moved his gaze up her limp body to Nanao, who was smiling down at Katie.

"That was a big one," she said. "How did you like it, Katie?"

"——……"

No answer came. Katie basked in the afterglow, her mind lost in that light. A sign the treatment had worked, overcoming any resistances. Her nervous condition had been neatly resolved; by the time her mind returned, she'd feel far better, as if born anew. That may not arrive until after a good night's sleep.

Oliver pulled his hands back out of her clothing and stood up. A wave of fatigue hit him, like his shoulders were made of lead. It almost crushed him, and he could barely speak.

"…My part here is done. Sorry, Nanao…can you…?"

"I can. I'll join you when it is finished. Clear your mind as best as you can and wait for me, Oliver."

In response to her kindness, he turned his back and walked away, almost crawling out of the room. When he stepped through the door, Chela and Pete both rose to greet him.

"…All done? Good," said Pete.

"How is Katie faring?" Chela asked.

The obvious question. Not looking up, Oliver managed an answer.

"She's recovered. Just like you wanted."

Without meeting Chela's eye, Oliver turned and headed for the

other bedroom. He did not want to exchange another word. His stiffened shoulders made that clear, and yet she tried to follow.

"Wait, Oliver. Can we talk—?"

"Don't touch me!"

A vehement rejection. He had never directed anything this harsh her way, and Chela froze—but before she could recover, Oliver was through the door. Her outreached hand caught only air. Sighing, Pete moved to her side; this was exactly what he'd feared would happen.

"Yep, he's *pissed*… Can you handle it, Chela?"

"…How could I?"

Tears were spilling down her cheeks. Without another word, Pete wrapped his arms around her.

In hindsight, this was the only possible outcome. She'd achieved her goal as a mage—and, in return, deeply scarred a friend.

CHAPTER 4

Dissent

Time had passed since the great sage Rod Farquois arrived. Their fearless antics were now well-known and sending ripples through the student body. What had, at first, been viewed as the prattling of a loon was gradually garnering genuine enthusiasm.

"And I'm saying the moment shit spread *under* the second layer, it was already a faculty job! A place the school doesn't even know exists, tackled by students alone? That's absurd! There's no telling what the hell will crawl out of those depths!"

"That applies to anywhere mages fight! How can someone too chickenshit to plunge into the unknown even call themselves a Kimberly student?! A coward like that oughtta fuck right off to Featherston."

Furious debates raged across the Fellowship. And not just in one location. Watching this from the side, in cute ladies' attire—the student body president, Tim Linton.

"They're all fired up," he said with a snort. "Are those critical of the faculty part of this rumored Farquois faction?"

"Yes, their ranks are swelling quickly in the lower forms," Miligan replied, shrugging. "Many of the underclassmen aren't confident in their ability to defend themselves, so Mr. Lombardi's mess hit them hard. Debating the merits of allowing students to explore uncharted territory, insisting the great sage was right to go to the rescue—and by extension, arguing the way Kimberly's always done things is problematic. That's the main thrust of their views."

To the council members, this situation posed a conundrum.

"And those views align with our attempts to impose order on the labyrinth," Miligan added. "I'm much more ambivalent about the fact that it's bolstering Farquois. Their behavior is far too provocative for us to outwardly support. Right as we were improving lines of communication with the faculty through Instructors Ted and Dustin."

"...Yeah, no matter how fired up they get, if Farquois's head rolls, it ends there. Otherwise, they're just a sub on a temp posting; when the year's up, they'll ditch Kimberly for good. You'd think that'd be enough to convince anyone it ain't gonna do no good making noise—but the great sage's charm means they ain't exactly being rational."

A pointed reminder of how thorny that mage was. Tearing his eyes off the lowerclassmen, Tim turned to go.

"I ain't about to let this run us ragged. The Watch keeps our distance from Farquois. Their bullshit plays into our goals; we'll take advantage of that—but if we gotta make contact, it goes through Instructors Ted and Dustin. The great sage is likely a handful for them, too."

"Agreed. I have concerns about the Gnostic Hunter headquarters' desire to unseat the headmistress, but that mess is outside the reach of us students. Leave that to the faculty, while we focus on campus and labyrinth security."

Miligan and Tim walked away. Their direction set, but their concerns still real.

"Here's hoping Farquois doesn't rock the boat any harder," Tim growled. "But something tells me they're only just getting started."

Earlier that same morning, the Sword Roses were by a painting leading to the labyrinth for a very unusual reason.

"Let's head in. Our destination is the Library Plaza at the far end of the third layer. I'm sure you all know the way, but caution is in order. The lesson upon our arrival is the real goal here."

With that word of warning, Chela leaped into the painting. A moment of darkness, and she was scanning her surroundings before her feet even touched down. She sensed no immediate threats, so she turned to face the comrades following her.

"Oliver and I will lead the way. Pete, you and Katie stick to the middle. Nanao, I'm afraid I'll have to ask you to guard the rear."

"And guard it, I shall!" Nanao grinned.

Chela assumed that meant she'd taken the hint and shot her a grateful smile. They formed ranks accordingly and made swift progress through the familiar ground on the first layer. For a while, no one spoke. Eventually, Chela decided the moment was ripe and glanced at Oliver.

"In our fourth year, labyrinth lessons are a fact of life. Assembling at the scene is very Kimberly. Wouldn't you agree?"

"Yeah, it is."

A very curt answer, with no further discussion forthcoming. After last night's events, she'd expected this, but she failed to still the ripples it caused within her. He'd never once been this cold toward her.

"Um, Oliver…I know it may be a bit late, but—do allow me to apologize for last night. Clearly, I did not spare enough consideration for your feelings on the matter. But if I may offer an excuse, I have my reasons—"

"Apologize for what? I agreed to it, and you don't need to feel guilty. You owe me no apologies, and if my attitude afterward is bothering you, put it out of mind. I am mostly just lashing out."

Oliver cut off her defense—a response even harsher than she'd feared. Chela gulped, then tried once more.

"'Mostly,' meaning *not entirely*? So therein lies a failure on my part. If we could talk—"

"We can't and won't. Drop it, Chela."

"……!"

He ended the conversation without allowing her to fix a single thing. She knew better than to pursue it further.

Observing all this from behind, Pete sighed. "…Hurts to watch. She should have given him more time. It was only yesterday; obviously, he's not ready yet."

Running next to him, Katie bit her lip. Oliver's treatment last night had helped her make a full recovery, but inside, she'd processed none of this—and what she'd just seen only gouged the wound. It was her fault there was friction between them.

"I've never seen Chela this upset..."

"Don't you go joining her, Katie. We're in the labyrinth now. And just to be clear, this is one-hundred-percent Chela's fuckup. None of it is on you."

Pete was quite firm on that. Katie very much appreciated his words, but she was still hurt. Since last night, she had not spent a moment outside her friends' care. She knew she should be less of a burden, but every effort to escape this came back to haunt her. Katie was out of options—and though well aware she was at a standstill, suffering from it, Pete turned his attention elsewhere.

"Yo, Nanao."

"Hrm?"

Behind him, Nanao raised a brow. Pete was not addressing her with his voice, but via a mana frequency only she could hear. He continued talking, not letting Katie know.

"Just asking out of curiosity—absolutely not trying to criticize— but I'm wondering why you didn't stop things last night. I'm sure you could guess how Oliver would take it, and I doubt this was just priori- tizing Katie's recovery."

This had been on his mind all night. Chela's proposal had effec- tively ensnared Oliver, but Nanao had held a card that could easily have freed him. If she had simply argued in favor of Oliver's emotional state, Chela could not have pressed the point. Yet, Nanao had taken no such action and allowed the scenario to unfold. That seemed rather out of character.

It took her a while to respond. Long silences were also not like her.

"...Groundwork must be laid. That thought has been on my mind for some time."

"Groundwork...for what?"

"For the event of my demise. Should that happen, I wish to smoothly hand Oliver off to Katie."

That answer nearly made Pete's eyes pop out of his head. Yet, he got it. This was no impulsive thought, but a course she'd arrived at after lengthy consideration.

"I know not when or where this may happen. You know that yourself, Pete. Naturally, I am not inclined to throw my life away. I swore a vow to you all accordingly," said Nanao. "But I am a warrior, and I know this to be true—when the time comes, my turn will not linger behind. I will die before a single one of you."

"......"

Pete ran on in silence for some time. Would that he could argue, but this decision was so very *her*. While he was fumbling for words, Nanao continued:

"And by extension, with my death, I would leave Oliver bereaved. Should that happen, I would want him free to turn to Katie. Last night was a step in that direction. That is how I saw it, at the least."

"...Okay, yeah, that adds up."

Pete sighed. The source may be different, but the final conclusion was rather like Chela's own. Nanao wanted Oliver and Katie closer to ease the pain of her death—and she was convinced that moment *would* arrive, be it sooner or later. For that reason, she'd accepted last night's events. She knew it would cause frictions but was certain it would be to everyone's benefit in time.

"...I said I wasn't criticizing, but I take it back. I'll give you a nice long lecture about this one later. And..."

"Mm?" Nanao crooked her head.

She had imagined he'd rebuke her for this revelation, but apparently, he had other thoughts in mind. Of course he did—about himself, not Nanao. She didn't know yet that Pete arguably bore a larger burden of guilt than Chela.

"...give me a briefing on how seppuku works. I may turn out to need it."

"You will?!"

That shocked her enough to use her real voice, not the mana frequency. Katie looked back, puzzled, and Pete spoke up to distract her.

"Guy'll be waiting up ahead. Don't you go acting all gloomy where he can see. You can come to me for whatever you need."

This was aimed to hide that Pete and Nanao had been conversing in secret, but he meant every word of it. Tears formed in Katie's eyes, and she quickly wiped them away.

She was well aware she was in no state to talk to Guy, but she at least wanted to be in better condition than she was now.

Beyond the marsh they'd once crossed to rescue Pete, they found a crowd of fourth-years waiting. By the looks of things, nearly two thirds of the students were already there, gnawing on rations, quenching their thirst, waiting for the start of class as each saw fit. Farquois was standing at the back, but to everyone's surprise, Theodore had joined them. There seemed to be slightly less tension between the two, so Oliver assumed Theodore was there to ensure the great sage did nothing untoward.

The five Sword Roses waited a good ten minutes before Guy showed up. He was in a party of five headed by Valois, who was flanked by the Barthés and Mackley—a frequent grouping as of late.

Guy waved at his old friends; Oliver kept a close eye on Pete's response, but he just snorted and let it pass. Oliver was relieved to see him disinclined to pick a fight.

Another twenty minutes passed, and nearly everyone was present. Seeing that, the great sage smiled and stepped forward.

"Everyone made it on time. You are fourth-years—diving this deep is hardly a challenge," they said. "Now then, today's class shall make use of this Library Plaza. We'll be re-creating records from the Library of the Depths' forbidden tomes for educational purposes. Simply watching would be a drag, so there'll be some hands-on lessons mixed in. I am here, so you will return home safely, but do try and take it seriously."

With that, Farquois held up a hand, clutching a thick volume. On Oliver's previous visit, the reaper guarding the gate had overseen this reenactment, but it sounded like this time, Farquois was choosing the scene. Kimberly faculty were allotted a set of additional privileges over active labyrinth functions, and use of this location must be one of them. Aware of what might follow, Oliver glanced at his friends, and all braced themselves.

"Let's begin. *Volsek Streets.*"

At his call, a few dozen pages flew from the book, swirling in the air above. As they did, the surroundings abruptly shifted, and the group found themselves standing in a rustic town. Storefronts with barkers outside, ox-drawn wagons, women drawing water from a communal well—ordinaries going about their lives. A pastoral sight, and Gui and Mackley both sounded baffled by it.

"...A small town?"

"Deep boonies."

"Guards up. A gate could open in the sky any second," Lélia said, raising her athame.

Nearly every student was poised for combat, which made Farquois giggle.

"A fine attitude. But for this chapter, you need not worry yet. This is my class—I would not throw you into battle unwarned. I will explain things one step at a time," the great sage began. "First, this takes place eight hundred years before the Great Calendar began. In other words, before the series of events that led to the Union as we know it. Links between mages rarely crossed national borders, and most lived with the ordinaries, like villages mages do today. A simple life. Most were less of the ruling class than they were advisers, offering guidance."

Walking through that past, the great sage spoke. The view around them shifted to another part of town, where an elderly mage of yore was healing a wounded ordinary. Still a sight one saw from time to time, but compared with the emphasis placed on the privilege of the ruling class, Oliver felt this mage seemed far closer to the villagers around. Perhaps some would call this the good old days.

"And it goes without saying that Gnostics existed even then. Those cast out of society, without a place to call their own, have always sought salvation from the outside. And no matter the day and age, it fell to mages to deal with that threat. Though, their numbers were far fewer, and ordinary soldiers played a far greater role."

Again, the view shifted dramatically. The peaceful streets were filled with soldiers wielding swords and spears, roaring as they charged into the fray. They were fighting humans—presumably Gnostics—mingled with kobolds and goblins. A mage was in command, wielding a wand at the back of the army, barking orders, and casting powerful spells at critical junctures. A very different style of combat than they saw today—and Farquois saw frowns on their student's faces.

"Starting to wonder, yes? How could *this* handle the threat? A few mages, but primarily ordinary soldiers—in your minds, hardly a force capable of repelling any tír invasion. Threats so great, our best mages often give their lives to stop them—how could an ordinary contribute anything? That's what you've been taught, and it's accurate to the threats of today."

Everyone was nodding at the assertation, but it didn't match what they were seeing. These soldiers were clearly putting their lives on the line against the Gnostic forces—but to the students' eyes, it was all so *tame*. No waves of tír creatures overwhelming them. No gate open in the sky, raining *things* that might not even count as living. The only signs of gnosticism were a few humans or demis with altered body parts. In which case, yes, an army like this likely would suffice. A tough fight, but little different from wars between opposing groups of humans—no need for a dedicated unit of Gnostic Hunters.

"But turn the clock back far enough, and a time like this did exist.

Far fewer mages than there were today, yet they were enough to keep the world safe. Why do you think that was? Was this quality over quantity? Were each of them absurdly powerful?" said Farquois. "Hardly! Certainly, there are any number of magical techniques lost to the march of time, but in terms of pure combat potential, we are far more powerful than the mages of yore. The speed of technological advancements only accelerates the more people there are to study them. Everything learned through our bloodstained history has made us stronger. That is beyond all doubt."

Farquois was answering the questions on every mind. There were certainly times in which ancient mages were lauded, and in specific ways, those reputations were well deserved—yet that did not refute the general trend of technological improvements resulting from the advances of time and population expansion. All the ancient cultures that had risen and fallen in days gone by could not begin to match the sum of modern Union power—a commonsense view. There were certainly theories out there arguing against this consensus, but few in the magical world took them seriously.

"So how was it these ancient mages were capable of holding the line? The answer is simple. The Gnostic threat was far smaller than it is today."

Farquois made this sound obvious. And it lined up with the evidence before their eyes. Ancient Gnostics were weaker than modern ones; thus, they required far fewer mages to stop them.

"I'll add this is not merely Gnostics. The regular tír migrations were nowhere as frequent as what we see now. And the scale of them was much smaller—it was extremely unusual for anything to cross over that could cause legitimate damage to human populations." Then Farquois asked, "...Doesn't that strike you as odd? They had far less opposition back then compared to now. If they had invaded at full strength, our world would have stood no chance. And yet—it's almost as if the tír gods were waiting for us to *grow*."

Farquois flashed a grin. *Terrifying*, Oliver thought. He could tell where this was going, yet he found himself listening with rapt attention.

"Naturally, that's not the case. The tír were not reluctant to invade us properly; they had good reasons why they could not. You could say the conditions were not ripe. And they are now—thus, the invasions are formidable. So what *are* these conditions? There must be a reason why the threat is so much greater than it was then—but what could that reason be?"

Most of the students could guess. But that's exactly where the great sage went off the rails.

"The number of *prayers*. The more people are left behind and seek salvation outside our systems, the more prayers the tír gods receive. And that unseen accumulation leads to the gates connecting our world to the tírs. This is why the ancients never faced invasions on modern scales. They simply had a far smaller population in the first place— and thus, the total number of Gnostics never crossed the threshold." Farquois went on: "Naturally, this number rises and falls with the stability of society, but are there no Gnostics under good government? It's hardly that simple. The population expands accordingly—we must be mindful that the ratio and sum are separate figures."

"Wha—?"

"Uh, that's not…"

"One moment, Mx. Farquois," Albright said, raising his head as shock waves rippled through the crowd. His brow furrowed even more than usual. He was clearly speaking not just as a student, but as the heir to the man in charge of the Gnostic Hunters. "Apologizes if my ignorance has caused a misunderstanding, but it feels like what you've said is a dramatic departure from conventional wisdom. My understanding is that the tír threats have increased in frequency over time due to a corresponding increase in their proximity to our world, and because the tír gods themselves have a mounting will to invade us. In other words, they're coming to us—that is the accepted theory held by most astronomers."

"Generally speaking, yes. And it's a crock of shit. A cockamamie fabrication, a web of words spun for the convenience of the society in which we live."

Farquois's harsh words only made Albright grimmer.

A stir ran through the crowd. And as the mood grew ominous, the great sage turned toward their silent colleague.

"I plan to continue in this vein. Any objections, McFarlane? Or do you intend to silence me?"

"...Suit yourself," Theodore said, eyes closed. "As long as you cover the required content, Kimberly allows all teachers to fill the remaining time as they see fit. Even if you choose to pad your lessons with pointless flimflam."

At a glance, this appeared to be a neutral stance, but Oliver could tell that was his only option. If he acted to silence Farquois here, that would only be giving their arguments credence. Emphasizing that this was an inconvenient truth kept under wraps. To avoid that impression, Theodore could take no action.

Farquois knew that perfectly well, and with that answer, they turned back to their students. No one here could stop them.

"I have permission, so let's get back to it. I called it cockamamie, but it stands to reason you all believe it. It's a difficult point to *prove*. Are we inviting them, or are they coming to us? Arguably, either theory describes the same facts. In the past, this was the subject of vehement debate; at the time, the factions were referred to as the invitation theory and the proximity theory. For a variety of reasons, the former fell out of favor, and few today are inclined to revisit it. A sad history in which the truth is buried in darkness."

Farquois hung their head despondently. A theory that had likely gone unvoiced at Kimberly for ages—but the great sage was not done yet.

"That said, I realize it's hard to accept. The whole world trembles before the rising Gnostic threat—and this argument means it's a part of autointoxication, a byproduct of the magical world itself, the very definition of an inconvenient truth. We've swelled our population heedlessly and, to feed them all, have enslaved countless demi-humans, working them to the bone, offering no assistance to those preyed upon by this society, and simply abandoning them to their fates. Those sacrifices are all viewed as fuel to the fires as we seek ever greater successes in pursuit of our spells. A society like that is *bound* to drive people to gnosticism. As their suffering mounts, so do their prayers, and thus, the gates from tírs grow ever larger."

As they reached that conclusion, they drew their wand, chanting a spell. A number of graphs appeared in the air above the students' heads. A diagonal line rising, and below it, another set of numbers rising in tandem.

"Back to the truth behind both the invitation and proximity theories. If we simply reduce them to the numbers on record, which theory is correct is as clear as the sun is bright. The number of Gnostic incidents, the number and size of gates that open—all directly proportionate to the expansion of the Union and its population. Well? Do you see which theory makes more sense now? This is far more tangible than chalking it up to the unfathomable will of the tír gods."

Backed by the statistics, Farquois urged understanding. As the students studied the graphs, wavering, Andrews raised a hand. Faculty or sage, no Kimberly student would ever swallow something unchallenged.

"If I may, Mx. Farquois. No one here can prove you haven't altered these figures to fit your argument. And you collected this data yourself, I assume? There are some clear discrepancies from the figures I've previously been familiar with."

"Ah, well spotted, Mr. Andrews. You've got the prior knowledge to avoid being easily taken in. Yes, you're right. The graphs I've prepared have some dramatic differences from the official figures released by the Gnostic Hunters. Naturally! They're *manipulating* the figures before release. Carefully and thoroughly, to ensure nobody has a basis to revive the invitation theory."

Farquois's smile was rather bitter. Andrews had expected just this argument and took it in stride, but the great sage's tongue was still wagging.

"The numbers on these graphs come from my personal information network. Specifically, they're provided by apprentices spread throughout the Union. If you insist I can manipulate them as much as I please, I can't refute that. But—if I don't gather my own numbers, we'll never have accurate data. After all, our own society does not want this to be true. No official numbers are reliable. The only numbers I can trust come from people I know—with their feet on the ground."

"I respect the logic of that, but what basis do *we* have to trust it?" Andrews asked, not backing down. His question implied that no answer could convince him this man's claim was anything but a delusion.

Seeing their student steadfast, Farquois nodded. "You clearly need more evidence. But…do the others?"

They glanced across the sea of faces. Andrews flinched, turning to get a look for himself. Farquois was one of the world's few great reversi mages, and their speech was far more than mere words. Regardless of the content, the fact that Farquois themself was speaking carried unnatural weight.

Andrews's humbling experiences in his first year had proven the springboard to fortifying his own mind—and he had been unmoved. But not all students here had such defenses. Even in close range, Andrews could see several who had clearly been captured—and while they might not yet be Farquois's puppets, they'd evidently taken a big step in that direction. Andrews turned back around, glaring fiercely at them, but the great sage merely shook their head, smiling.

"No need to get worked up. I'm not expecting you to believe it here and now. I merely ask that you file my claim aside in a corner of your mind. For one thing—just because I'm a proponent of the invitation theory does not mean the content of the class to come will change much. Sad to say that does not in any way mean you *don't* have to fight the Gnostics."

With that, they raised the book again. Feeling a shift in the atmosphere, the students quickly braced themselves anew.

This was no time to dwell on the sage's words. They were already on a battlefield.

"Let's begin. Assignment one: The Monster Rock that Fell on Geshele."

Certain they were ready, Farquois plunged into the heart of their lesson. The scene around them shifted three times, and they found themselves in another time, in another place, on another street. The ordinaries in these ancient records were all looking up. Spotting a gate yawning above, every student blanched—and as they watched, polyhedrons rained down, each with over fifty faces.

"You can feel it, yes? Like the migration you witnessed last year, these hailed from the Uranischegar of old. Considering the great conjunction next year, this is the first type you'll need to learn to handle. Give it your best shot."

At Farquois's word, the battle began. The fourth-years split into front and back lines, and the latter divided the territory, drawing magic circles on the ground, erecting barriers—matching the defenses used in last year's migration.

The great sage smiled approvingly. "Mm, mm, excellent. Being extra cautious of the risk of corruption is never wrong. But if you're too defensive, that'll limit your movements. Don't forget their first action will be to expand their territory."

They were well aware of that. Students with faith in their damage dealing were out front, and Guy, who usually hung back, was moving aggressively with them. Dice with too many sides were rolling their way—and each time a side hit down, the ground beneath it changed. The faces they imprinted folded up, connecting swiftly into new objects.

They were copying themselves—a fact that made him shudder. Guy threw out some toolplant seeds, spreading their cursed roots. Like thorns coating the ground, snaring the polyhedrons, slowing one after another down. Between the curse's strength and Guy's magical inter-ference, they could not corrupt this soil as fast as ordinary ground. And once pinned down, the other students' spells rained down upon them.

"Heh, effective application, Mr. Greenwood. Against something this unnatural, it should be hard for you to locate an effective con-duit for the curse. But if you attack with cursed toolplants, you need not change your fighting style. Not picky what they target—a reliable technique."

Farquois was calmly evaluating things, but even as they spoke, poly-hedrons were breaking through the concentrated spellfire, bearing down on the fourth-year formation. Like with the migration last year, Uranischegar's minions proved exceptionally resilient to damage that altered their shapes. For that reason, most students resorted to other spell types...

"Gladio!"

...but Nanao's *iai* spell cleaved through five polyhedrons in a single swing. The students behind her winced. Compatibility with her target be damned—this was all her exceptional mana output and the sheer sharp edge on her severing spell. Anyone could tell just how beyond the pale that was, and indeed, Farquois folded their arms, snorting.

"Nothing fazes you, Ms. Hibiya. No matter who or what you're up against, you fight the same way. Children like you embolden those around you and diminish the fear of the unknown. A joy to have you on the front lines. Though it reminds me of someone vexing."

The sage pursed their lips, and their phrasing nagged at Oliver's mind. There was no time to dwell on it now, however—he was firing spells at a group that had wheeled around the pack ahead. As he did, Pete's miniature golems were flitting about, making noise and cast-ing lights near the enemy. These polyhedrons had no obvious sensory organs, and he was testing to see what made them respond. Surmising as much, Farquois spoke up.

"Mr. Reston, testing with golems is fine, but careful about making

contact. Corruption has been known to happen through a familiar. Auto is preferrable to remote, and if any get caught, immediately cut the channel. If anyone else is using familiars, take the same precautions."

Pete immediately switched up his golem's functions; Mistral had been using his splinters along similar lines and quickly pulled them back. The battle raged on, the fourth-years' spell barrage refusing to let the enemy close in. Their swift action at the start paid off, halting the polyhedrons' initial offensive and leaving them helpless. Students were using convergence spells on the shattered fragments, making sure all parts were melted in their flames.

"Just over eight minutes to annihilation," Farquois said, folding their arms and grinning. "Perhaps too easy for you. Oh, right—you're all *formidable*. Let's skip a few stages. Assignment Two: The Day Kuan Harbor Fell."

The pages of the forbidden tome danced, and once more, the view shifted. Now they were in a large port town. People were loading and unloading sailing ships, and an even bigger gate appeared in the sky above. The fourth-years sprang into action, and Farquois watched with delight.

"I didn't plan to throw this at you today, but I'm pretty sure this is the limit to what you can handle. Don't worry—no matter how it goes, I am here."

Naturally, no one banked on that promise. The core stance carved into every Kimberly student's heart and mind sent them hurtling into the fray.

There were quite a few close calls, but in less than an hour, they fought their way to victory. The Library Plaza reverted to its original form, and the fourth-years were all alive, if badly out of breath. Farquois went around, swiftly healing the wounded; a few had been corrupted, but since this was merely a reenactment, it left no lingering effects. This cleanup took little time, and before they knew it, everyone was of sound mind and body.

"Excellent work. Right, that's enough for today. A reward for making it through—I'm sure you're starving."

Farquois waved their wand, and enough lunch baskets for all came sailing in from who knows where. The students hesitantly opened them up and found baguette sandwiches loaded with colorful fillings, and a congratulatory message written out in condiments on top. A stark contrast to the rough battle, and they had to laugh. As the tension finally drained away, everyone started eating. Not a common sight at Kimberly, which rattled the Sword Roses—but then a friend strolled up, lugging his basket.

"Free lunch? Here? Talk about generous."

"Guy." Oliver gulped, turning to him.

Oliver was torn between the desire to burst into tears and to apologize profusely—but logic barely kept him from either. They each took seats in a circle and dug in.

"Sorry I kept away during the fighting," Guy said, savoring their proximity. He bit into his sandwich. "Didn't dare take my eyes off that group. Mackley was loud as hell, squawking and wailing, 'I'm doomed!' every few— Ow!"

A rock hit the back of his head, falling to the ground. Putting a hand to the bruise, he looked back to see Mackley scowling over the Barthés' shoulders at him. He hadn't expected her to be in earshot.

"She got ears in the back of her head?" he said, wincing. "Uh, anyway, figured I'd at least eat with ya. Wanted to see how y'all are doing."

"Mm, yeah, of course," Oliver replied.

He managed a nod, taken aback. He'd caught a glimpse of some unfamiliar friendships and was rather conflicted about it.

Guy looked away from Oliver, checking each friend in turn before settling on Katie, who was very obviously trying to hide behind Pete. Sensing a weird vibe rippling out around her, he frowned.

"Y'all are gloomy as hell," he said. "None of you are even trying to hide that something happened. What, you guys have a squabble about the brownies I left behind?"

"Yeah, no, we split those evenly," Oliver said. "Each of us is savoring the final morsels."

"There's no replacing your desserts. Come back to us and bake some more," Pete demanded.

This curt behavior showed no changes in their affection.

Guy closed his eyes, nodding. "I'd like to think I'm making progress. Sorry it's taking so long."

"You have nothing to apologize for," Chela said. "But know that all our thoughts are with you."

Guy smiled—then refocused on the friend acting least like herself.

"…So? What's up with you, Katie? You a bur on Pete today?"

"Let her be. She blew a transformation spell this morning. Gave herself a great big bushy beard, doesn't want you seeing it."

"…I did not…"

Pete's story was so appalling, it forced Katie to pop her head out from behind him and deny it. That alone reassured Guy, so he took another look around. He hadn't spoken to them in far too long. Not just Katie—he could tell things were strained among the group. Unable to work out why, he sighed.

"…I guess a lot's happened. I wasn't there, ain't gonna dig further now."

"We don't want to cause you any concern, really," said Chela. "Not to change the subject, but you've found yourself a new crowd. Ms. Valois, the Barthé twins, and Ms. Mackley? I realize you were with them in the lava tree mold, but—"

"Yeah, and once you get to know 'em, they ain't that bad. I can't get much thinking done on my own, so it's a big help. Right, Annie?"

"Hold this for me, male twin. I gotta knock a bitch over."

"Sit, Mackley!" Gui yelled over his shoulder. "Guy, quit winding her up!"

Mackley had her wand half drawn, and Gui quickly restrained her.

Guy shouted back an apology, to which Oliver commented, "You fit right in. A relief…and yet I'm also jealous, if I'm honest."

"Oh yeah, Oliver? You miss me that much?"

Guy crossed his arms, making a joke of it, but to his surprise, Oliver just nodded gravely.

"I do. It's like the biggest light in the room burned out. Really drives home how much you warm my heart and illuminate the darkness within."

This sounded so sincere, it took Guy's breath away. He could tell Oliver was fighting back tears. Ordinarily, Oliver would never let himself look this fragile, so it struck home. Before he knew it, he was reaching toward him—an unconscious reflex to embrace a friend in need. Catching himself in time, Guy balled up his fist, punching himself in the face.

"Guy?!" Katie yelped, leaping to her feet.

"…That was close. Could've been real bad."

"What are you doing? That was so loud! Did you break a tooth?"

Chela pulled her wand to heal him, but Guy was on his feet, back turned. He dropped his half-eaten sandwich back in the basket.

"Sorry, I'm not handling this well, either. Gonna pull out before I slip up," he said. "Oh, but first: Extruditor."

Guy fired a spell over his shoulder as he left. Oliver hadn't been braced for that and went flying right as Guy had visualized it.

"Huh?"

"Oliver!"

Chela caught him on reflex. In her arms, feeling her warmth on his back, Oliver gaped after Guy.

Guy turned his head halfway around, giving them a sidelong glance.

"You're the ones fighting, right? I dunno what's going on, but you patch that shit up. Drawing it out don't do nobody no good. You two have been on the same wavelength since day one."

With that parting gift, he stalked away. Unable to speak, Oliver just stared after him—and Chela kept her arms tight, like she was loath to let him go.

"——......"

"...Chela..."

He heard a choked sob. She was crying into his back, and that robbed him of words once more.

Staring at them intently alongside Nanao and Katie, Pete ventured, "He's right. You don't have to forgive and forget—but at least chew her out, Oliver. You've punished her enough. Ain't nothing harder for Chela than you shutting down around her."

The same went for Pete, so he knew this was best approach he could take. Oliver had no response; he just sat listening to the sobs behind him. What reason did he have to make Chela cry?

As that thought settled in, the emotional gridlock he'd been left in following the previous night began to grind again at last.

Once they'd reached the first layer, the others headed up to campus, while Oliver and Chela alone went to their hidden base. They might miss the first afternoon class, but neither cared. It was clear to both what their priority was.

Together, they moved wordlessly to the living room and sat down on the couch without even making tea. There was a very long silence. Unable to find words that sounded right, Chela abandoned her attempt and wore her heart on her sleeve.

"...Um, Oliver. I don't know what to say."

"Don't force it. Let me say my piece instead."

He took the lead. In his mind, he already knew what to share with her. He had just been readying himself for that during the silence. Saying this out loud took a lot out of him.

"There's something you should know. Something...I'd prefer you keep to yourself, not a word to the others. So far, only Nanao knows."

"My lips are sealed. I swear on our Sword Rose," Chela said, hand to her heart.

Oliver understood this was her solemnest vow and meant more than any contract possibly could. Putting his faith in it, he nodded and took a breath.

No need to tell her the whole story or any details. Just a summary of the salient points.

With that in mind, his lips made to speak.

"I was forced into unwanted sexual relations. While still young. Family reasons," he began. "And—the daughter resulting from it perished."

"——!"

Chela's face froze like she'd been hit by a blizzard. Doing his absolute best to keep emotion from his voice, Oliver pressed on.

"This is why I'm resistant to sexual contact. And why I was so insistent on contraception in our second year. I don't want any friends of mine to suffer like I did. This history makes me incompatible with typical sexual practices for mages. Even if there is logic to it—no, *especially* if the argument is a logical one—my body and mind viscerally reject it. This is why last night's incident got to me."

There, his admissions ended. All too brief considering the events involved, but Chela's reaction showed she got what he needed her to know. She had a strong imagination and knew how to speculate with precision. What he'd said would let her fill in the rest. Even without the fine print, she'd know the unspeakable grief and horrors that had beset him.

"…That's…awful…"

An agonized gasp escaped her. She was forced to reevaluate last night's events—flipped by a single blow. A witch's victory turned to a memory of the highest cruelty she could inflict on a friend.

"…I feel as if I finally understand the true meaning of the phrase *an unpardonable sin*. How badly I hurt you, how deep the cut must go, how cruelly I twisted that knife…"

"Don't go too far with that. The wound was already there. You simply got your finger caught in it unawares."

"Ignorance is not an excuse! Not with something like—!"

She broke off before she could shriek.

Chela had realized she was in no position to get emotional and restrained herself. Her heart rocking like a ship on a stormy sea, she forced herself to think. What could she do? How should she face the wounded heart before her?

"...That's hardly fitting. Beating myself up for it will just make you miserable. Give...give me a moment. Not to ease the burden on me, but to choose words for you."

With that, she buried herself in her thoughts, well aware this was an insurmountable problem. No true comfort could be found, and even knowing that, it was hard to truly be there for Oliver. Apologies and condolences would serve no purpose. So what should she say? In light of all potentials, what could she do?

In time, she reached her answer. No better options presented themselves, no matter how she fought.

Therefore, she merely needed to descend to the depths in which he stood.

"...I'm done thinking. And gathering my nerves."

"___?"

Her tone sounded weighty, and Oliver wasn't sure why. Chela turned toward him, her eyes like mirrors to his—and she took a step down the stairs to the abyss below.

"I have an admission of my own. It may take a while, but I'd like to swear you to silence as well."

Those few words made it clear what Chela was asking; to her, this was tantamount to flinging herself upon the pyre.

Oliver realized she was not saying sorry or trying to cheer him up but attempting to restore balance. In other words—offering up a history as grim as what he'd shared.

"I swear. On our Sword Rose."

The same vow she'd made. Chela nodded—and began.

Approximately nineteen years ago, in a house so ancient that its history was longer than Kimberly itself—the McFarlane manor.

"Hoh-hoh, hoh! My, my... A sight for sore eyes indeed!" an elderly witch said with a cackle.

They were in a medical ward, protected by every manner of magical barrier, the elemental density in the very air carefully controlled. The witch was washing her newborn great-granddaughter. The baby's ears had been pointed at birth but were now rounding themselves off.

"...Undoubtedly a half-elf. And a rare morphling! Even I have never encountered one outside the pages of a dusty tome. And for it to be a babe that carries my blood, bathed for the first time by my hands..."

Her voice was filled with joy and exaltation. Pulling the infant from the bath, the midwife dried her off and wrapped her in swaddling cloth, reverently offering up that little bundle to the mother. To the very woman who'd brought elf blood into the McFarlane clan, now lying exhausted on the birthing table.

"Well done, Mishakua. Birthing this babe does the McFarlanes—nay, the magical world—an enormous boon. Perhaps you will live to see the results of—"

"Hold your tongue, child."

With a word, the witch was silenced. Not another person in this family would dare speak like this to her—but even the head of the McFarlane clan could not talk back to Mishakua. The elf had been a mage far, far longer. In a meeting room, perhaps the witch could have wielded order as a shield, but at the moment of this child's birth, no one had labored harder. A dash of rudeness provided no excuse for protest.

"You had to make it hard for me," Mishakua whispered, smiling at the fussing baby. "Was my belly that comfortable? You were far too reluctant to leave. We almost had to cut me open to get you out."

Here, her gaze turned sideways to her husband, who'd said not a word through these proceedings.

"Hold her, Theodore. While I make amends to my ancestors."

"......Mm."

Theodore nodded stiffly and took his child in his arms. Seeing the fear behind his eyes, Mishakua repressed a smile. He'd barged alone into her home village yet betrayed no such emotion. This was a man long past fear of death. And yet—what he held now reminded him of what that emotion felt like.

"......?"

As he stared at the baby, the terror in his eyes gave way to tears. A fact that flummoxed him. Seeing her husband at a loss to explain these tears, Mishakua saw right through him.

"You love her, right? Despite it all."

That choked Theodore up.

This was not his first child. More children than he had fingers bore his blood. Yet—he'd not been permitted to treat a single one of them as his own. They were children of branch houses, and Theodore was never their father.

He'd grown accustomed to that process. Forgetting to fret over it, no longer letting it get him down—and so he'd been sure he could not love. Even if he finally got a child to call his own, he'd been sure his heart would remain frozen over. And from the moment he learned his wife was pregnant, he'd feared nothing more than holding this tiny body in his arms and feeling nothing.

How wrong he'd been. It rocked his world. The moment he held his daughter in his arms, all the emotions he'd bottled up came spilling out. He was allowed to love her—and that fact alone made tears gush down his cheeks, splattering on the baby's face. Mishakua smiled at the sight of it.

"That's how it should be. If you cannot love me, love her instead. Love her for all the children you cannot," she said to him. "What's her name? You said you had one in mind."

She spoke like a teacher collecting homework. Holding his child in shaking arms, staring into the baby's face, Theodore answered:

"…Michela. I chose a name reminiscent of your own. And…"

"Ah. For once, you outdid yourself."

Mishakua grinned and held out her arms. Theodore nodded, knowing what that meant. He handed the baby back to her.

Cradling the tiny body in her arms, the elf who'd ventured into human land whispered to her, "I am sorry, Michela. You've been born into a cruel world. You may loathe me for it all you like. But I *do* love you. That fact cannot be changed."

She held her close to her heart. No matter how cruel a fate the future held, the love they felt here was real.

The laws of the world granted elves exceptionally long lives, but the speed at which they grew was no different from humans. Half-elves like Michela were the same. A few years from her birth, she'd grown a lot, and like all children did, she took an interest in anything and everything around her.

"Do I not have any brothers and sisters, Father?" she asked one day.

Theodore was relaxing on the living room couch with her and smiled awkwardly.

"…A difficult question. One could say you do, and one could say you don't. Our family is a little unusual."

A vague answer, and he picked her up. It was morning, and her ringlets were freshly set. They swayed as he held her.

Catching an anxious look on her face, he asked, "Are you lonely? Being an only child?"

"No, not at all. I have you and Mother," she replied. "But—if I do have brothers and sisters, I thought they might be lonely."

Innocent kindness that broke his heart. Love and sadness welled up within, and he held her tight.

"You're so nice, Chela. I don't deserve a child like you."

"Why not? You're always nice, too!"

Knowing nothing, Chela smiled. A smile without a cloud in sight. Theodore wished she could remain ignorant forever, all too aware that was a fragile hope.

Chela grew up bathed in her parents' love, but on the day she turned eight, her great-grandmother deemed the moment ripe. She took the child to her workshop—to tell Chela about the purpose a McFarlane heir with elf blood must fulfill.

"Do you know what this list of names is, Michela?"

Chela was seated at the table, and the ancient witch unrolled a scroll before her. Looking at the list of names inscribed upon it, Chela crooked her head. All she could tell was that these were likely all male names.

"These men all have reservations on your womb. In time, you may have a child with them. Commit their names to memory—you'll meet each in turn soon."

The witch's tone was as measured as that fate was harsh. Chela considered these words, trying to match them with what she knew.

"...You mean fiancés? One of them will be my future husband?"

That was the best interpretation she could manage. At her age, that was an admirable grasp on things, and in another household—that would have been the right assumption. But her great-grandmother shook her head, chuckling. This was the McFarlane household, a place far removed from norms.

"What an adorable mistake, Michela. I'm afraid this list contains no partners. If you take a liking to one, you can snare him if you wish— not many would refuse you," the witch said. "But simply put, you must share your blood with them. These are children of households chosen to help spread elf blood in the world of man and ensure it *lasts*. Naturally, we've taken their individual behavior into consideration. From this list...you've already met the Andrews boy, yes?"

Chela remembered a boy her age she'd met not long ago.

She'd tried talking to him a lot, hoping to be friends, but after they'd compared spells before the watching adults, he'd grown very stiff. She didn't get why, and it made even less sense that she'd make a child with him one day. But her great-grandmother wasn't waiting for it to sink in.

"There have been very few half-elves in history, but you are not the first. Yet, none of those previous mages were able to leave a lasting bloodline. There are several reasons for that, but simply put—they never managed to make their blood set in. Very few humans are able to get an elf pregnant. It requires a high level of magical aptitude for their aspects to properly mingle."

Chela was aware of this history already. Including the fact that she was the only complete half-elf known to exist in the magical world. Elves and humans could not easily breed, and even if they succeeded, the children were often functionally lacking—and incapable of reproducing.

The higher the magical potential of the human, the milder those issues became; Theodore met those conditions, and so he and Mishakua had managed to produce Chela. She understood that she was being asked to do the same thing. And thus, she at last realized what this list meant.

"Most old houses would try to keep the blood to themselves and repeat the errors of the past. But not the McFarlanes. Mindful of those failures, we renounced our claim on the blood and elected to aggressively loan out your womb. Process this fact and prepare yourself. Be ready to bear a child for every man on this list."

This witch was not hiding anything. She told her great-grandchild that quantity would compensate for the likely rate of failure. For this reason, she would need to have as many children with as many promising young mages as she could. A purebred elf could bear very few children in their long lives, but half-elves had human advantages and were not limited by that. She made it quite clear Chela was ideal breeding stock.

It added up. The logic of it was sound. Understanding it as best she could, Chela nodded, far too young to imagine the toll it would take on her.

But despite her youth, she had concerns. Specifically, every name on this list hailed from a house of some repute. Even if not all succeeded, odds were high that many would produce offspring. That would leave her with husbands and children outnumbering the fingers on her hands. Even if mages had no rule against polygamy, these seemed excessive.

"I understand, Great-Grandmother. But I do have one question."

"What is it? Ask anything."

"With this many, I don't think I can love them all. I think that will make the children very lonely. What should I do about that?"

Such an innocent question—the witch could not stop herself from laughing. Not at the child before her—but at the parents who had raised her.

They'd coddled her far too much. Teaching her kindness and consideration would only make her suffer later.

"You don't yet understand, Michela. Love has no part of this. Each house will handle such trivialities on their own, and frankly—it doesn't matter. We must establish elf blood in the world of man. No other concern can compare," the witch explained. "If this doesn't make sense, look at how your father lives. Men and women have their differences, but his path is much like yours. Watch him close, and you will work out how you should comport yourself."

Baffled by her great-grandmother's words, Chela nodded. Nothing she knew of her beloved father matched this speech at all.

Her great-grandmother swiftly made arrangements, and the opportunity soon arrived. The day prior, Chela's father had grimly told her to accompany him, and so Chela visited an ancient home at his side, unclear as to what this visit meant.

"Now this is a surprise. I did not imagine you bringing the girl on everyone's lips."

Chela and her father were seated across from a witch in a parlor that spared no expense. A strong incense tickled her nose, but not unpleasantly; the herbal tea and tarts on the table before her, too, gave off a scent that was excessively sweet. Chela felt out of place here. This was no ordinary welcome—a fact that she sensed, even if she could not discern the nature of it.

"It was not my decision, but my grandmother forced it on me. She's a smart girl and won't make a scene. Assume she's here to learn the ways of the world."

"Naturally, she's a welcome guest. Though, I cannot guarantee this is an appropriate education… Heh-heh, what a darling child. I imagine you've taught her things, but I can tell she does not yet understand. How long as it been? Since anyone this innocent set foot in this house?"

Eyes on Chela, the witch smiled enchantingly. Odd how she was not remotely tempted to smile back, Chela thought. She took a sip of tea, and the flavor of it made her frown. Theodore silently took the cup from her hand and set it back on the table—not wanting his daughter to drink a brew designed as a functional aphrodisiac.

Wetting her lips with her own tea, the witch stared long and hard, as if searching for how to entertain this company. After a moment, she asked the obvious question.

"…Do we show her everything? If that's why she's here?"

"Let's not get ahead of ourselves. Like I said before, I don't plan to stay long today."

"Such a shame. And here I was all prepared. Still, I'd rather not take her into the bedroom with us."

With that, the witch stood up, moved around the table, and sat down on the other side of Theodore. This seating arrangement befuddled the child. But as she watched, the witch ran her hand up Theodore's neck and smoothly placed her lips on his.

Theodore did not budge. Chela's eyes went wide, and after a long kiss, the witch pulled away with an alluring smile.

"Then let us talk a while," she said. "If you're not staying long, can we at least share a drink?"

She pulled a hand from her hip and a set of a liquor bottles and glasses flew from a shelf in the back. She placed three glasses on the table, uncorked a bottle, and filled two of the glasses with liquor. The third, she filled with grape juice, a modest consideration. Her father began talking to the witch, wearing a masklike smile—and Chela watched them as if this was a scene from a far-off, distant land.

A bewildering time passed, and once evening fell, Theodore wrapped things up and took Chela away. She had so many questions, she didn't know what to say. As they walked in silence, they passed a man at the main gates.

"____"

Somewhat older than Theodore, the man scowled at the sight of him. Theodore ignored that entirely.

"Evening, Mr. Walpole," he said. "Apologies for greeting you on our way out."

"…No matter. I had not intended to see you at all. At least you didn't stay the night."

With that, the man quickly sped on past. But a few steps beyond, he turned back, his voice laden with fury.

"If you're done here, begone. What look did my wife wear to butter you up, McFarlane stud horse?"

This hit Chela hard. She didn't grasp the meaning of it but could tell from the man's tone this was an unbearable insult. She started to turn, but Theodore tugged her hand, leading her away. As if letting these words taint his daughter's ears was far more unbearable than the insults themselves.

When the manor was out of sight behind the hill, they drew to a halt. Chela looked up at her father, whose face betrayed no emotion.

"Father, was that—?"

"Sorry, Chela. Let me wash my mouth out first."

Talking over her, he pulled a potion from his pocket and swirled it around inside his mouth—as if he could not bear the unpleasant sensation clinging to him otherwise.

Chela watched, waiting. At last, the bottle was empty, and he put it away.

Theodore looked grimly down at her. "I'm sure you've worked it out. I must share my blood with the woman we met; that man is her husband. The act itself is yet to come, but there are stages to work through. Connections between houses are always a chore."

He sounded tired. She'd guessed as much but, with that confirmation, reconsidered what she'd seen. Even from the sidelines, she'd sensed no pleasure there. Thus, she could imagine just how unpleasant it had been for him—and what that meant for her own future.

"...So someday, I'll be like you were today?" she asked.

"You won't have to go to them. I like to brag about how light on my feet I am, so I make the trip, but given the repute of the McFarlane family, it's more appropriate for them to come to you. There is no need to be friendly and please them—that is *their* task. If you are not inclined, you may merely sit there in silence, sipping your tea."

Theodore spoke in a flat tone, perfectly aware that would be no comfort at all. If his daughter was the type of mage who enjoyed treating people like dirt or bewitching them with her charm, that would be one thing—but those qualities were as far from Chela as could be. Yet, that did not free her from the obligations of her blood.

Their positions were different, but the witch earlier was much the same. Her duty was to capture Theodore and bring profit to her house; her feelings on the matter played no part. She was used to it, but he could not know if she enjoyed it. Perhaps the distinction had long since ceased to matter. The more of a mage you were, the more that was the case—as Theodore himself knew all too well. He'd been known to act accordingly.

Theodore turned, gazing at the ordinaries' town set against the hill, drenched in the light of the setting sun. Chela followed his gaze. The beauty of this view was the sole saving grace, as far as he was concerned. It prevented this precious time spent with his daughter from being an entirely unpleasant one.

"My role in this is partially a penalty. I made a big mistake once and must share my blood with more than other relatives. Grandmother is still furious with me. My mistake led directly to the miracle of your birth, yet still, she cannot get over it."

Theodore's eyes reflected the reddening sky.

Over time, Chela had gathered that her parents had not exactly met peacefully. She'd never once thought to ask about the whole story. That wasn't what mattered to her. She had a dad and a mom, and they both loved her.

But she had long nursed some doubts in her mind, and she took this moment to voice them.

"...Two questions, Father."

"Yes? Go ahead."

"I know that you don't like that woman. That you were here out of duty as a McFarlane. But—why is it you don't love Mother?"

He looked down to find tears in Chela's eyes. Theodore pursed his lips. Not surprised. He'd known this question would come eventually.

"That's a hard question," he said. "I respect her talents and her character; as partners, we get along fine. Just—if you ask if I can say I love her with the same confidence I do you…that's much harder for me. When I met her, I'd long since turned my back on such things."

This was not a question that could be answered in a word. Chela was smart enough to realize the truth was far more complex than she could yet understand, and so she fell silent. Pressing further would just make him suffer.

With some difficulty, she put her feelings away. Telling herself to be satisfied that at least he had not said he *didn't* love Mishakua. Theodore sensed all that and thus was infinitely disgusted with himself.

Why couldn't he answer her? That entire day, his daughter had not asked him for one thing.

"...Okay, then. The other question..."

Her emotions in check, Chela looked up at him again. Her gaze made him fear what was coming next. He felt as if another blow like that one would make him unable to bear being himself.

"...Do you need a smoke, Father?"

The absolutely last thing he'd expected. It took him several seconds before an awkward smile appeared on his lips.

"...Well, isn't that a surprise? I've never smoked in front of you!"

"I've smelled it on you sometimes. Always when you seemed unusually unhappy."

Chela gave him a sad look, like she was ready to cry—and Theodore scooped her up into his arms, well aware this hug was an escape.

"No need for that. I'm with you right now. As long as I can get a hug from you, all my bad feelings go away. I only smoke when I *can't* do that."

Despite his inner turmoil, the platitudes came out all too easily. But he could not let this discussion end there. His feelings didn't matter. Those were never worthy of consideration. All that mattered was his daughter before him.

"Chela, my darling daughter."

"Yes?" she said quietly.

He could tell she knew this next part would be important. Knowing it made him a terrible father, he said it anyway.

"You're a smart girl, so I'm sure you know. You will never get to love or have a family in any normal way."

"...I know."

Chela nodded slowly. Neither frustrated nor upset about it. A fact that made Theodore's heart ache all the more.

A child this wise and kind, and I'm throwing her to the pits of hell.

Pushing her onto the path of a spell that will lead her far from human happiness. That truth can never be changed. So at the very least—I can only hope she will find a light to shine upon that treacherous descent.

"If there is hope—then hope for good friends. That alone, we are allowed. If nothing else."

His voice shook. Once, he'd had a light of his own. Those words carved themselves deep into Chela's heart, showing her where to place the love she had. In bonds where the value of her blood did not exist, where her heart was allowed to be merely human. Only precious friends were allowed that—and thus, she sought that future more than anything.

"And that's *my* origin story," Chela concluded, allowing herself a small sigh.

Oliver was just staring at her in silence. She'd never imagined she'd reveal any of this, not even to friends. A past that lay beside her, deep within. But sharing it had been the sole means of remaining friends with Oliver—if she'd kept it under wraps, she'd never have been able to meet his eyes again.

"…Your past is, in a sense, my future. Despite the similarities, there is a fundamental difference. And it's all too clear how that difference led to where we stand now," Chela said. "Simply put, I *adapted* to it. But you rejected it and are fighting it even now. That's the long and short of it."

Her voice rasped. Facing each other's darkness shone a light on this discrepancy.

His past was a wound still bleeding. But she no longer even viewed hers as painful. Her heart had grown up with a piece missing, and now she acted as if that had always been her nature. And for that reason, she'd hurt him. She'd blinded herself. By asking him to match her, she'd wounded him all over again.

"One thing fell into place. I wasn't drawn to you just because we stood in similar depths. That alone is likely matched by any student from an old house. It's clear to me now—I was drawn to you because you were desperately trying to keep your feet on the ground within those depths. That's something I unconsciously peeled off and cast away—something you're still clutching close to your chest."

Chela revered that. She could not begin to call it hope. What he held on to was a corpse, one that would never breathe again. He knew it would never answer, but he could not stop himself from calling out to it, loving it.

And for that reason, she wished only to put her arms around both.

"May I—hug you, Oliver? If I still have that right."

She spread her arms, and Oliver nodded, moving closer and leaning against her. Chela felt as if a huge missing piece snapped back in place. She couldn't lose this. It was too precious to her to ever let go of again.

"...You matter so much to me...," she whispered, trembling.

Oliver's arms closed tightly around her. Leaving no gaps between them, as if staving off the chill winds. In the hopes that this could satisfy her, if even for a moment—just as he had always done.

He'd kept them waiting *too long*. Seeing Oliver in that last class had made that painfully clear to Guy.

Clearly, he'd been too optimistic. He'd only once seen his friend in that bad a state—back in their second year, when he'd been in the throes of that mystery slump.

"""""""Ah-ha-ha-ha-ha-ha!"""""""

"Ngh...!"

In a dimly lit curse wrangler workshop, Zelma's cursed dolls assaulted Guy, scissors and razors in hand. Bisque dolls in frilly lace, cackling wildly—an unsettling sight, but Guy fought them off with puppets made from the cursed wood of his toolplants.

A basic training exercise on the use of familiars, but not an easy one.

Zelma's automatons were unsurprisingly powerful, but what ran rings around that was the law of curse conservation. Each hostile doll he felled meant that much more energy stored in his own puppets.

"...Tch...!"

It was hard enough to operate familiars fueled by his own curse energy; the more *alien* energy they acquired, the more likely they were to escape his control. Mindful of the puppets' individual capacity, Guy was pulling appropriate levels of energy from them, wrangling that within even as the fight raged on. If he lost control of a puppet, it would all be over, but if he siphoned too much energy away, the puppets would lose the battle. This was an exercise designed to press home what a two-edged sword fighting with curses was, but...

"I ain't getting stuck here!"

Riling himself up, Guy used a cursed wood puppet as a decoy, and while the hostiles were focused on that, another of his familiars bound both arms into a single club, swinging horizontally. That crushed two foes at once while the third hostile sliced up the decoy and spun around—but the excess of curse energy slowed it down. Guy had been counting on that and pressed the advantage. His wooden puppet tackled the foe, knocked it over, and trussed it up—and the roots dug into the hostile doll's body.

"Ah-ha-ha-ha-ha-ha! Ah-ha-ha! Ah-ha! Ah-ha-ha! Ha!"

The invasive roots destroyed it from within—and with nothing left to power it, the screeching laugh was silenced. The doll crumbled away. His familiar was hit with a blast of curse energy, but Guy collected that before it could escape his control. It was virulently unpleasant, but he let it in without fighting it, soothing the energy, settling it down—and when that was over, he allowed himself a relieved sigh.

"What, already done?" Zelma blinked. She'd been reading on the sidelines. "It's only just past noon. This was a full-day assignment!"

"Haah...haah... I ain't got time for that! Gimme the next one, Instructor Zelma!"

The thrill of success driving him, Guy swung around for another go.

"At least you're motivated," she said, shaking her head. "But I'm afraid I can't."

"Huh? Why not? I'm ready for more!"

"I can see that. It's assignments I'm short on. I neglected to mention this was your final exam."

Guy locked up a second, not quite processing this. She flashed a grin at him.

"Knowledge, technique, and attitude—you've got everything a wrangler needs. The Warburgs are a house of wranglers, and I'd stake my name on it. I knew you were moving fast, but to get here in less than a month? I can see why Baldia was after you."

She clearly felt the same—and that helped it finally sink in. Guy was already at the goal line he'd been racing to get to.

"...So I'm done? Then..."

"You can assume you've reached the minimum threshold for living a normal life with curse energy in you. You know how to stop it from transmitting, and what to do if it does—you've mastered that body and mind. All you need to do is make that routine. Naturally, that doesn't mean you live like you did before you were a wrangler— but you should be able to recover your friendships to an extent. Here's where you're grateful to me."

That last was a joke, but Guy's eyes were filling with tears.

He could be with his friends again. He couldn't touch them, and he definitely couldn't hug them, but he could at least be around them and *talk*. That did evoke gratitude—and so he voiced it.

"Thank you so much...!"

"Hmm, sincerity is always welcome. That said, you made such smooth progress that I didn't really manage to wind you around my finger. Shame! And here I'd planned to lure you away from Baldia... Still, your preternatural self-control gave you this outcome. I'll have to satisfy myself with knowing I helped bring a promising future wrangler to the world. Not calling this a prize for that, but in honor of your completed training, I do have a gift."

Zelma waved a wand, and the doors opened. Three mages stepped in. Guy knew every face—all three were Kimberly graduates who'd joined the faculty.

"...Gwyn, Shannon...and Rivermoore?"

"Mm, today's assignment was a bit of a challenge, so I had them on standby in case you lost control of the curse energy. You're a lucky man, Guy. No other school in the Union had multiple consolers this good, on staff but not full instructors. All credit to your own choice to attend Kimberly. That said, they *are* busy. Let's get this done, people. Your consolations should be able to quiet even this powerful a curse for a full week."

"On it." Gwyn nodded and put his viola under his chin.

Rivermoore took a seat at the piano, while Shannon sat Guy down on a chair, her hand on his shoulder.

"Let me...touch you, Guy," she told him. "Don't worry. Just...relax."

"Er, um..."

Guy was baffled, but they were already playing. The music stole his attention away, and he stopped squirming.

"Listen close—no need to answer me," Zelma said. "Instructor David came to me the other day. Said with your talents, a binary choice was cruel and unusual. Wondered if there was any way to give you more time. I found that hard to spurn. I owed him for his help cleaning up the mess Baldia's apprentice caused; even as her proxy, that's not a small favor. And I also didn't want to see you repeat Lombardi's mistakes."

As the gentle melody washed over him, Shannon overlapped her zone with Guy's, consoling the curse. It felt far too comfortable. The tension drained from him.

"To be more specific," Zelma began, "twice a month, you'll be getting consolation from this crew. That'll render the curse inside you temporarily dormant, and during that period, you'll be able to act almost as you did before becoming a wrangler. Essentially an unorthodox way to keep both fires burning. Half the time, you'll be able to relax around your friends and look after magiflora. Perhaps the outcome will be stunting your growth in both fields—but I'm betting you'll deem that a small price to pay."

Guy nodded, stunned. Sensing this was hard for him to believe, Zelma backed it up.

"I should add this is preferential treatment even by Kimberly standards. It's a testament to the hopes we're placing on your talent—and a reward for bringing everyone stranded in the lava tree mold back alive. Deaths down there would have been a thorn in our side. A solid standing for those who wish to tear the headmistress down. Heh-heh—like I told you before, just *being alive* makes curse wranglers worthy. You were no exception to that rule."

A flash of her patented wit. And at last, it started to feel real. The concert played on.

"Ironic—Lombardi forced that curse upon you, but your choice to be his Final Visitor is what earned you this treatment. Perhaps some other event would have led to you becoming a wrangler, but no other impetus would ever have allowed you to split your time. Your enemy, and your brother in curses—and without ever knowing him, he gave you much." Then Zelma added, "…I often think there's little difference between a blessing and a curse. Both entwine themselves in the fabric of the world, altering fate. Once you've swallowed it all—where will it lead you?"

A tear escaped Guy's eye. Zelma turned away.

"Enough of my noise. Give yourself over to the racket inside and out, Evil Tree. And accept that moniker. It may feel like a curse—but it's just as much a blessing."

With that last admonishment, Zelma left the room. Everything but the beautiful music faded from his mind, and Guy gave himself over to it.

Epilogue

The night after Zelma arranged a three-mage consolation, Guy returned to his rightful position, sharing the good news with the Sword Roses.

"Ah…"

The entrance opened with a spell, and he stepped inside, taking it all in. The couch he'd sat on so often, the table his books rested on during cramming sessions, the kitchen he knew his way around with eyes closed. The pleasant light of the crystal lamps, the incense Katie had burning—to his very skin, all aspects of the workshop felt like home. How could they not? He'd spent so much time here over the ages.

"…Feels like I've been away for years, but it wasn't even two months."

"Hmph, subjective—but I bet it felt longer to me," Pete grumbled, stepping past and then turning to face Guy.

Nanao and Chela stood beside Pete, smiling.

"Each day an eternity—how glad I am to see you returned, Guy."

"…Yes, you made it back. Back to us…"

There were tears in Chela's eyes, and Guy winced, shrugging.

"Like I wasn't gonna eventually. How could I just abandon you all? Is there some other Guy I dunno who was born without a heart?"

"…Are you sure you never considered it? Not even once?" Pete asked, staring into his eyes.

Guy puffed up his chest, holding that gaze. "Not even *once*. I mean it. Logically, sure—I was aware the option existed. But that ain't even worth considering."

He remembered that talk with Mackley and the Barthés. They'd helped him a lot while he was separated from the Sword Roses. He intended to keep that connection alive. But not once had he been tempted to switch to their side—and thus, that was his answer.

Pete smiled and moved closer. Comforted, secure, he buried his face in Guy's chest.

"Then good. Rub my head. I'll grant you special permission."

"Okay, sure. You've really learned how to wriggle in," Guy said with a snort. He began mussing Pete's hair, keeping that up till the boy was satisfied.

Then at last, Guy turned to where Katie stood in silence by the door, at Oliver's side—an awkward distance between them.

"C'mon, Katie. I dunno what went down, and I ain't gonna ask. Whatever it was, it don't matter. I knew that from the start. How about you?"

Katie's shoulders quivered; she was unable to budge under her own power. Nanao quickly moved over to her, took her hand, and led her to Guy. Once they were too close for Katie to flee or hide, her eyes met Guy's, and something burst within.

"…Uwahhhhh…!"

She let out a wail and flung herself at his chest, rubbing her face on him. Guy's arms locked around her back, pulling her in tight. Each of them had longed for this but had been unable to indulge. The heat they'd so missed provoked a sob from each.

"…Damn, you're warm. Were you always like this?" Guy muttered, feeling the thaw inside.

He'd have loved to stay like that forever, but he reluctantly pried his arms away after a couple of minutes. It had to be done—he knew the deepest freeze here was not his heart or Katie's.

With all his love, he mussed up Katie's hair—then turned away to face Oliver, who'd barely kept his emotions from showing this whole time. Oliver told himself to put on a welcoming smile and stifle any conflicts within.

"…Welcome back, Guy. I really—"

"Get that phony smile off your face. I can't bear it."

Guy didn't even let him finish. And that shattered the mask over Oliver's heart. The false smile twisted up, and his lips quivered, deprived of their next words.

"...!................!"

"Uh-oh. Okay."

Unable to watch, Guy grabbed him into a bear hug. Oliver didn't even try to resist, his body cold as ice.

Trying to warm him with his body heat, Guy whispered, "I'm good with all of it. You know that. I gave you permission. I dunno *what* it was, but that don't matter. I forgive *you*."

He piled that on, not an empty word to be found. In fact, Guy had a pretty solid idea what had happened between his friends. Oliver and Katie had maintained a delicate closeness, and he'd been the buffer between them—his lengthy absence would inevitably make that come tumbling down and leave them both with a burden of guilt.

So before anything else, he needed to make them set that down. For a while, he rubbed Oliver's back, then he cupped his cheeks, pulling his head up. Face stained with tears, eyes and nose red. And that cleared up the last snarl inside Guy.

"...Ah—"

He was certain now: He'd come back to stop *these* tears.

And at the same time, he realized his feelings for Katie were not the least bit pure. When he had her in his arms, his thoughts were with someone else.

"...I'm as nuts as the rest of you," Guy muttered, his fingers brushing away Oliver's tears. One hell of a messy relationship he found himself in, but he chose to view that as proof he belonged in the Sword Roses.

He didn't want to be *normal*. They'd come too far for that, and it was much too late.

He squeezed Oliver once more, even tighter than before, only letting go when he was sure the boy's sobs had died away. Guy was convinced and prepared. There was nothing more to think about—he could be himself again and feel great about it. He stalked over to the cupboards, yanked open the doors, and inspected where his baked goods ought to be.

"You ain't got *nothing* left in stock, huh? Cake is one thing, but you ate your way through all those cookies and biscuits?" said Guy. "Right then, let's make one of each. Katie, don't just stand there, gimme a hand."

"Oh—r-right!"

That snapped Katie out of it, and she ran over. From that moment forth, everything was normal again, and they all went about their days. Pete flopped down in a chair with an open book. Chela put the kettle on, lining up teacups for everyone. Nanao was at Oliver's side, and the two of them settled in on the couch.

"...Oh...," Katie murmured, using a wand to pour ingredients into a bowl.

"What?" Guy said, working next to her. In the same workshop again. "Something fall into place?"

"...Yeah, I think so," she replied with a nod. Her hands kept moving, but she looked at him, voicing her discovery. "You're just like me, Guy."

"......"

Guy smiled. He didn't even need to nod; that had always been the bond between them.

They both were enamored with the same man. Their hearts held captive by the same source. In which case, it was best to share those emotions with each other. Remembering Pete's word of caution, Guy made up his mind to do just that. An awkward relationship, never quite siblings or romantic—from today on, he had a name for it: *cohorts.*

"Get all three types of flour mixed right. Texture's way different if you slack on that."

"Mm, I remember it all. How many times have we made this together?"

Katie smiled, doing her part—and Guy doing his, in perfect harmony. It had been far too long since the group saw them like this.

Watching from the couch, her arms around Oliver, Nanao whispered, "See, Oliver. You have not lost a thing."

"...Yeah...it's all right here," he said tearfully, nodding.

Steam rose from the cups Chela poured. Every now and then, they heard Pete turning a page. The scene in their workshop just as it had ever been.

"So he came back, safe and sound? Sorry it took so long," said Gwyn.

The day after Guy's return, Oliver was at his cousin's hidden workshop on the first layer, sitting across the table from them and reporting in. When he was done, Gwyn looked rueful.

"We could have quieted the energy much earlier," Gwyn added. "But that's not a real solution, and we thought it best for him to learn how to control it first. After discussing the matter with Instructor Zelma, this is how things turned out."

"Yeah, so he said. Twice a month for a while, at least. Brother, Sister, I really appreciate it. I'll have to say the same to Rivermoore."

Oliver took pains to mention the contributor not present. And that name prompted a rare bit of mirth on Gwyn's lips.

"Heh, he seemed pretty pleased with it. He feels indebted to you. And this favor does little to repay it. When you get a chance, assign him a doozy of a job."

His grin had shifted to wicked—and Oliver winced. Aware of how her cousin felt, Shannon added milk to his tea, smiling softly.

"Cyrus's piano...is so gentle. I do...love hearing it."

Oliver had to agree with this assessment. He'd heard Rivermoore's consolation concert in the Kingdom of the Dead and vividly remembered how astonished he'd been by that delicate, merciful melody. At the time, he'd been confused by the contrast between it and the man's behavior—but the way that incident played out and how he'd acted on campus ever since had vanquished all doubts. Oliver knew Guy was safe in his hands.

The conversation died out, but Gwyn did not immediately bring up the next subject. Oliver was well aware of what that would be. Not one recent meeting had ended without it getting touched upon.

"...Given the politics on campus, I'm glad your crowd has settled down. Farquois's behavior is far beyond what we predicted. They brought up the invitation theory in class? That's not bold; it's insane. Not that I don't get the value in arguing that at Kimberly, but..."

Gwyn rubbed his temples, sighing. Oliver knew exactly how he felt but drew attention to the thing he could not look past.

"But what they said is *true*. As we well know."

Gwyn and Shannon responded with grim silence. Oliver took a sip of tea, then searched for any signs of life behind him.

He found her soon. And if he did, she must want him to.

"I'd love to see your face, Teresa," he murmured.

Without a second's pause, she appeared on her knee before him.

"I am here, my lord."

"Mm, thank you. Have some of these. They'll melt in your mouth," Oliver said, pointing to the cookies and pulling out a chair.

Teresa sat down right away but did not reach for the cookies, though he knew she liked them. Oliver searched her profile and soon understood.

"Something on your mind, I see. Close at hand—Ms. Appleton?"

"——!"

He got it in one, and she looked shocked. Oliver smiled, and Shannon added a scoop of sugar to Teresa's teacup. If she would not take a cookie, then perhaps this should be sweet.

"I can tell. Not many people would worry you outside this table. And her recent actions have not gone unnoticed. I only saw her briefly myself, but I saw enough to hazard a guess. She wants to pull Guy away from us? No—she wants to make him hers."

From the pieces he had, he assembled a theory. Teresa's silence was confirmation enough, and so he addressed the conflicted emotions within.

"If you don't report that, you're shirking your duty to me, but if you do, you'll be betraying her. You're caught between those two motives?"

"...How...?"

"Because I'm thinking of you, even when you're not around," he said. "On my lap."

He turned on his chair, patting his knees. She slipped off her chair and into his arms. Making close eye contact, Oliver spoke gently.

"Long story short, I'm not planning on meddling there. It's only natural people outside the Sword Roses will fall for him—and not just Guy. People have feelings for one another; that's a part of the world, and I would never dream of forbidding it."

"......"

"That *would* change if Ms. Appleton took drastic action. Too strong a charm, attempting to eliminate competition, etc. But I'm not worried about that now. I have faith Guy will tackle the issue head-on, and her previous behavior tells me enough about Ms. Appleton's character. And...I know I can trust the friends she's made."

Realizing that included her, Teresa quietly thought this over. That tickled him, so he gave further counsel.

"Don't overthink it. Just do what's right for her. Offer advice if she comes to you, listen to her grumble. No need to report every detail. You being a good friend alone will help her. And that will prove invaluable in guiding her to a happy ending."

Pushing her to be a good friend, to the appropriate closeness. He'd known Teresa needed that right now. Teresa thought about it a while, reached a conclusion, and unconsciously rubbed her cheek on his chest.

"...Then it's okay if I stay Rita's friend?" she whispered, a trace of a smile.

Sensing her relief and joy, Oliver returned that smile.

He'd never seen Teresa respond emotionally to an issue with her friends. Her fight with Dean or her clashing antlers with Felicia had both centered around *him*—but this time, she was driven purely by her feelings for Rita.

"…You've changed, Teresa. You're so much more expressive now."

"…Do you like me better this way?"

"It's not easy to compare. But I love seeing your heart grow. If only I could, I'd like to watch over that forever."

As he stroked her cheek, Oliver realized his slip.

Even making that wish was a sin. Because he was the one who was sending this girl toward certain death.

"…Sorry, I'm speaking out of turn."

"I don't mind."

Teresa shook her head, fully smiling now, and put her arms around Oliver's neck. Given how little time each had left, she knew "forever" was a cruel joke. But the wish itself filled her with such joy, she could almost cry.

A few days after the Sword Roses recovered their equilibrium. Oliver happened to be in the base already when Guy came bursting in, out of breath.

"Yo, anybody free?!"

"? What's up, Guy? I've got time, but I'm the only one here."

Oliver got to his feet, and that alone made Guy spin on his heel.

"Let's move! Before he's gone!"

Unsure what this was about, Oliver gave chase. A few minutes spent hurtling down corridors, and the answer to his questions came into view.

"Ah, you're back, Guy! You brought Oliver?"

"Oh?"

Oliver pulled up short, stunned. This man should not be here. He'd graduated from Kimberly several years back. Short of stature, but full of life—a trusted sight that made even the labyrinth's dangers falter. No less reliable now, and the rucksack on his back no smaller.

"…Walker? Why…?"

"Shocking, right?" Guy said. "I nearly lost my shit, too! He's headed into the depths, so I ran to see if anyone else was around. Dammit, wish the others had been there."

He ran his fingers through his hair in frustration. Meanwhile, Walker approached and slapped both hands on Oliver's shoulders.

"Been a while, Oliver! Guy was a shock, too, but you've grown so strong, I hardly recognized you! Yet—is it my imagination, or are you that much more brittle?"

"It's been far too long, Walker. I'm in peak condition, don't worry. But please—don't keep me waiting. What brings a graduate back here?"

The man's keen observational skills remained unnerving, so Oliver deflected.

"You heard of a labyrinth monitor?" Walker said, hands on his hips. "It's a standard position on the Kimberly administrative staff, and like it sounds, they're in charge of maintaining the labyrinth. I came back to take that job. I've been applying since graduation—my research on this place was far from done."

"Ah, so you're faculty now. Colleagues with Gwyn, Shannon, and Rivermoore?"

"Yep, I met them all! Gwyn and Shannon haven't changed a bit! But Rivermoore was a shock to the senses. Never saw him becoming a regular teacher! Ha-ha, all those games of tag I played with his familiars—sure takes me back. Maybe not the right phrase for it. Being here makes me feel like it was all just yesterday," Walker muttered, glancing around.

He'd infamously spent more time in the labyrinth than he had on campus, so that feeling made sense. After a moment, his gaze returned to his juniors.

"While their work is on campus, I won't get many opportunities to see you. That's a real shame."

"? Will we not bump into you down here?"

"Not so much, no. The labyrinth monitor role I took has been an empty slot for a while now—the extreme depth investigator. In other words, I'm in charge of looking into everything on the sixth layer and below. The difficulties and dangers are off the charts, so they weren't about to let a fresh-faced graduate tackle it—I had to get out there and prove myself a while. I figured it would take about a decade but somehow pulled it off while you were still here!"

Walker accompanied this with a carefree smile, but they could easily imagine how relentless a pace he must have set. The specifics were different—but the standards this job required were likely every bit as high as a Kimberly instructor. Achieving that in ten years would have been a feat—and Walker had managed it in a third of that time. He must have worked his head off, racking up accomplishments—and neither could imagine what.

"...The sixth on down? That's past where students are even allowed to tread. Well, except..."

"Yeah, that's where I got lost for the better part of a year. I swore I'd go back one day—no matter how many years or decades it took me."

"Mm, and didn't I say I was dying to hear more about it?" a new voice cut in.

Oliver and Guy jumped and swung around to find an instructor emerging from a side passage. A beautifully androgynous face above gaudy robes—unmistakably Rod Farquois.

"...Instructor Farquois."

"Oh, hey there, Mx. Farquois. Mm? Did you say that?" Walker blinked, crooking his head.

Farquois pursed their lips but soon recovered. "I did! I'm curious about your experiences, so I asked if we could discuss them at length—perhaps tonight."

"Oh yeah—I just assumed you were being polite. Sorry, my bad. My head was full of the labyrinth and my juniors!"

Realizing his blunder, Walker was all too ready to apologize, and that made Rod Farquois visibly flinch. For reasons totally lost on the Survivor. He was busy beaming and offering a suggestion.

"Hey! What say we chat a bit on the way to the sixth layer? I'd love the chance to show these kids what it's like, and they'll be safer with a teacher along."

"...Good lord. Not only do you ignore my invitation, but you also intend to turn me into a bodyguard?"

"Not up for it? Shame! We'll have to talk some other day, then. Might be a while—it'll be at least a month before I'm back on campus!"

With that boisterous promise, Walker turned his back. Oliver's and Guy's jaws hit the floor.

Farquois was on Walker in a flash, hand gripping his shoulder tight. "Did I say no? Bodyguard? Fine! I'll gladly take that on. No reason not to. It won't even make me break a sweat."

"That's the spirit! I'm counting on you!"

Walker swung back, took Farquois's hand, and shook it vigorously. The great sage's face was now actively twitching. Clearly the sight of a lifetime, and neither Guy nor Oliver dared to move. But at last, their minds caught up with the present.

"...Um, Walker?" said Oliver.

"You make it sound like...," Guy started.

"Yep, you two come along and check out the sixth layer! My privileges only let me take you as far as the entrance, and if you went in, you'd probably die, so this'll just be a quick glimpse."

A terrifying statement, but it certainly piqued their curiosity. The Survivor's offer made Guy and Oliver exchange glances...and then both nodded.

And so their motley crew's journey began. Farquois kept trying to ask about Walker's experiences lost below the fifth layer, and Walker was sharing effusively. However—even Oliver and Guy could tell the specifics were rather niche.

"It was all like that, almost nothing edible on the sixth layer," said Walker. "When the supplies I'd brought dipped below twenty percent,

I knew I was hosed. But I also thought—there's gotta be magical species that have adapted to this hostile environment. Maybe underground, where the changes are less dramatic—"

"Mm-hmm, that's fascinating. But it does seem like you're mostly talking about food. I'd quite like to hear about *other* things, too..."

Farquois was clearly getting impatient. Understandably—Walker had yet to speak about anything unrelated to food. Oliver and Guy were left sweating in their wake—and since the pace Walker set was demanding, they could not relax for a second. This might as well be a labyrinth trail run—and they maintained that all the way through the second and third layers. Before they knew it, they were at the Library Plaza. There, Walker's privileges let him skip the trial, and they sailed right on into the Library of the Depths.

"Hello, librarians!" Walker yelled right off the bat. "Don't glare at me like that. I'm not cooking dinner here again! Just passing through! Keep up the good work!"

The harpies flying around tending to the books in the tower, the reapers working the desks—every head turned to look. A clear distinction to how they reacted to anyone else—and Oliver remembered him joking about trying to make a stew here and nearly getting himself killed. If they still held it against him, then sure—that was so appalling, you had to laugh.

They raced across the plains where Oliver had once fought the philosopher Demitrio, and beyond that lay the Firedrake Canyon, where the mad old man Enrico had met his end. Observing the wyverns flying around their nests in the deep ravine, Walker glanced back at his juniors.

"You been to the fifth layer before? It's a bit soon, I'd imagine. Most need to be in their sixth or seventh year to make it this deep."

"...Not yet, no," Oliver said. The safe answer.

Not wanting to give anything away, he decided to follow Walker's lead as if this place was sight unseen. Meanwhile, it genuinely was a new experience for Guy, and his brow was deeply furrowed.

"Yeah, me neither," he said. "We're really crossing this? I'm not too confident."

"Oh, don't sweat it! You just gotta make sure the dragons don't spot you! And deal with it if they do! I once ran through here clutching a stolen egg!"

Walker brought a personal anecdote into it, but that was not in the least bit helpful. Oliver and Guy exchanged glances, and picking up on their nerves, Farquois sighed.

"Still, if we must move stealthily, four is a bit too many. Better we split into two pairs. I can handle anything here, but that should help the fourth-years out."

"Oh, nice idea, Mx. Farquois. You mind taking Oliver on? I had Guy under my wing before—wanna see how he moves these days."

"Wait, this is a test now? I ain't even been here before!"

Guy reeled, but they'd come too far to turn back. With the plan settled, they set out across the fifth layer. First, spells camouflaged them as they approached the canyon, and when the wyverns were away, they slipped on in. At the base of the terrain, Oliver quickly scanned his surroundings. The first thought on his mind was the lindwurm, but at least for now, he sensed nothing that large. Getting themselves spotted by that so soon would prove they had no business being here.

Once everyone was down, they began traversing the chasm basin. Wyverns wheeling overhead, small and midsize drakes scrabbling around the walls, and to effectively evade them all, the pairs frequently had to part ways. That left Oliver functionally alone with Farquois. And given that opportunity, he tried feeling the mage out. Starting with something that had been on his mind the whole way down.

"...Um, Instructor, you seem a touch different today."

"...Mm? Oh, you can tell? Yes, I'm a *liiiiiiiiittle* bit ticked off. Honestly, it's not often I meet someone quite as immune to me," the great sage grumbled.

Oliver was well aware they meant Walker; it had been all too clear Farquois was not holding the reins of their conversation. Their notoriously powerful charm was providing zero advantages in those interactions.

"He's a tough nut to crack. His core long since entranced by something else, no wiggle room for me to slip in. Ah, even admitting it out loud is humiliating! Such a humdrum excuse."

Farquois threw their head back, jaw clenched—a look you often saw ordinaries make. This rather threw Oliver. They'd always seemed so above it all, but their actions today were betraying the human within. Or perhaps that, too, was establishing a foothold for their charm.

As Oliver watched and pondered, Farquois suddenly turned his way.

"I could say the same thing for your friend Mr. Reston, though hardly to the same degree."

"Oh, Pete?"

"Yes. Other people being fascinated by me is the way of things, the natural order, but it's not often I get a snot feigning that fascination to get closer to me. It irked me, so I've paid him little attention. Honestly, a fellow reversi—I'd intended to look after him first and foremost."

Farquois shrugged, sighing like it was such a disappointment. But this statement caught Oliver off guard.

He'd long been concerned about the effects of the charm on Pete, but it had never occurred to him that Pete might simply be faking it. He couldn't necessarily swallow Farquois's opinion whole, but it was also a fact that Pete had his feet on the ground as a mage now. Ironic that this had worked against him.

Oliver felt his mind start to ponder Pete's motivations, but he soon realized that could wait. Whatever his friend's schemes, what mattered was Farquois's intentions.

"So you *were* planning on bringing Pete into your household?"

"Less a plan than…generally, that's just what happens. It's totally fine if he's an exception. The nature of this trait means reversi children are often profoundly isolated, and I've been plucking them all out of the muck. Mr. Reston simply wasn't in those circumstances. He gets more than enough love from all of you."

"......!"

That rattled Oliver even further.

It stood to reason the mage knew who Pete's friends were. That wasn't the issue; it was more the reason for all the reversi they'd taken in. Not a soul believed this was out of benevolence or sympathy—to the point where there was no use even paying lip service to those motives. Yet, voice them they did. Two possible explanations came to mind: Either Farquois took Oliver for a fool, or they simply didn't care about this conversation at all.

Instinctively, he felt it was the latter. But if that was all, then the feelers he'd put out were useless. Oliver wanted to take another step in, to catch a glimpse of their real intent. Couldn't hurt to try.

"If I might be a touch too honest—I cannot get a read on you at all."

He pulled up short, turning to face the mage. Sensing the shift in mood, Farquois faced him, too.

"Mm? Were you trying to? That's presumptuous."

"I think it's only natural. Your behavior is far too outlandish for Kimberly. And you know it—yet you refuse to change or even compromise. I don't know why. I can't tell what you intend to achieve with this performance, or what you really want. And without that insight, I've gotta assume you're a shit stirrer with a death wish."

He specifically chose strong language, scowling as he spoke. He'd felt this was a risky move, and it did earn him a sour look.

"Sounds like I've cause you much concern. Does my head look that easy to fell?"

"Hardly. But the headmistress's blade is not exactly dull."

"Fair enough. I'd go so far as to say there is no one else alive whose will is quite that sharp. After all, she's ruling over one of the world's keystones all on her own," said Farquois. "However—that is not a *human* job. It pains me to even look at her."

The great sage seemed unconcerned. The witch might claim their head the next day, yet they felt only pity for her. Oliver could say nothing back. Where he stood, blinded by vengeance, no amount of suffering could make him voice those words.

"You asked what I want, Mr. Horn? I'm not hiding it. If you want to know, I'll tell you now."

"——!"

That lead-in took Oliver's breath away. The next words would be decisive. Were they a mad mage not worth listening to, or would this speech contain a fragment of truth? His eyes strained to see the difference, and Farquois spoke softly.

"I want to change the world. Ordinaries, demis, mages—everything we consider *people*. Make a place where not one of them will be called fuel for the fire."

Who was asking, and who was answering—for a moment, Oliver lost track of it.

"An implementation and expansion of the civil rights beliefs. Rephrased in words the world can parse—that's essentially it. Nothing astonishing there, surely? Everything I've done and said before my students is in line with that thinking. If you simply take it at face value, I'd not even need to explain myself."

Stifling his leaping heart, Oliver tried to grasp the facts.

What was this? What was even happening? Was Farquois aware of Oliver's background and teasing him about it? In that case, he had to kill them here and now. Would that be possible, even with a spellblade?

Wait, calm down. Don't forget Guy and Walker are right over there. Don't rush into it—keep talking.

"That's…a stretch," Oliver managed. "There are too many contradictions. The great sage is a civil rights proponent? But the ultra-conservative Five Rods chose you, and you took that offer to come to Kimberly…?"

"Where's the conflict there? The Five Rods don't know what I'm after, and if they hear what I'm up to, they'll merely take it as a tactical disruption, a colorful performance. Frankly, they don't really give a damn what I think. All that matters is whether I'm effective in their efforts to topple Esmeralda—that's the only thing they have eyes for. Extreme tunnel vision."

Again, a note of pity in their voice. Oliver was watching their every movement, and that earned him a smile from Farquois.

"You wish to discern my motives and decide how you should act in light of that? I'll tell you—you need discern nothing and take no action at all. I will continue to act just as I have and ask nothing of you students in return. Fundamentally, I require no support or cooperation. Although, it *is* me we're talking about—people tend to like me even if I'm not making a conscious effort."

"……"

"Don't worry your head about a thing. I'll take care of it. I'll give you all a better future. But do know this: I am the great sage, Rod Farquois, and I will make it look *easy*."

Overwhelmed, Oliver just stood there. The great sage spun on their heel, moving onward. His mind refusing to budge, Oliver followed— and his ears caught a muttered remark, the mage talking to themself.

"...Angry the proof came late? Nay, you died too soon. I'm the one who should complain."

And these last grumbled words changed a doubt Oliver had long held to conviction.

This mage met my mother.

He wasn't sure how they'd met, but he was certain. He'd caught whiffs of it from their earlier behavior, and he was her son—he hadn't read this wrong. This was what had gotten under his skin so bad. Rod Farquois was acting like this due to the influence of Chloe Halford.

Oliver asked himself if there was anyone more deserving of trust. No matter how hard he thought, he could not argue that point. In his mind, his mother was just that unshakable a force. If he lined Farquois's actions up with his mother's, all his doubts faded. Act as he thought fit, as he felt right—just as Chloe Halford had always done.

Whether that was at Kimberly, whether that turned the Gnostic Hunters against her. And if the great sage was the same…

"____?"

This thought brought a new doubt to mind. Not about Farquois, but about Oliver himself.

Namely—was this mage not a better candidate to take on Esmeralda, the Gnostic Hunters, and the magical world itself? Were they not better positioned to pull off that epic feat?

Rod Farquois was a great mage. Everyone in the magical world knew their name—even if one only counted other mages, their followers numbered well over a thousand. A far greater number than those he'd earned through his mother's connections—and it was ghastly to even consider comparing their individual strength. When they claimed to need no support or cooperation, they were not exaggerating in the slightest. This mage had the strength to force the issue. That was why they could cheerily argue against the Kimberly way. Where Oliver could only skulk about the shadows, the great sage could show their face center stage.

This would end with their head rolling—he'd thought that prediction apt, but how dare he? Had he not the same concerns? How many brushes with death had he experienced on the path to those three teachers slain? Even Darius would have been formidable under other circumstances. Enrico had been a close call at the cost of many comrades' lives. Demitrio had been functionally a loss, overturned only by Yuri. Oliver could have died anywhere along that line. It was the devil's luck that he yet lived.

But what about Farquois? They were riling up the entire faculty yet stayed breathing on their own terms. Perhaps the other staff were talking Esmeralda down, but arguably, their actions depended on that. Kimberly was not a place you could survive on pure luck—had he not learned that lesson all too well?

"____? ____?"

Confusion made Oliver's feet falter. He knew this thought was too far-fetched.

But what if he just…left the rest to this mage?

That would be so easy. His comrades were already planning to sit back a year—why not do just that? Just wait around, and the answer would present itself. Either Farquois was true to their word and found a way to banish Esmeralda from the magical world—or they failed at that and lost their head, sowing discord between Kimberly and the Gnostic Hunters. Either way, he knew his comrades could turn that to their advantage. Simply put, as long as there was no risk of getting caught in the crossfire, there was no downside no matter what Farquois did.

Arguably, this would make his revenge harder to complete. But Oliver and his comrades had just concluded again that they could not prioritizing vengeance over the mission. And if he let Farquois act— then his comrades would be kept out of harm's way. He would not need to feed them to the pyre. He could keep his cousins from the flames of war. He could let Teresa's life last just that much longer—

"…Ngh… Haah…haah…"

His breathing shallow, Oliver walked on. A temptation too great to just shake off, giving rise to a desire all too desperate.

While Oliver's inner turmoil raged, the group advanced along the canyon. Two hours after their arrival, they reached the end of the fifth layer. A cave opened at the canyon base, and through that was a whole new view.

"Here we are!" Walker cried, audibly excited. "Up ahead is the sixth layer, commonly known as the Twisted Mountains!"

Oliver and Guy both gasped. This was a view that could rob anyone of words.

If one had to describe it, it was a range of mountains where up, down, left, and right had lost all meaning. An icy wind blew through it, constantly shifting directions, with such force that hill-sized boulders were caught up in it, tossed every which way. From their perspective, these boulders were floating, but that was not technically correct. The gravitational pull itself was constantly changing; everything was simply falling unpredictably. Only rocks in contact with the walls remained fixed. This meant there were mountains in all directions, and even those were warped into elaborate three-dimensional mazes. Not a trace of life anywhere—perhaps this place simply did not allow for it.

"...I've read descriptions of it...," said Oliver.

"...But it's even worse in person," Guy added. "All those dragons seem totally harmless."

Oliver forgot all other concerns, matching Guy's astonishment. This was clearly not a place either of them could possibly survive—and the fact that Walker was now *working* here really drove home how great his skills must be.

"Can I get an answer now, Mr. Walker?" Farquois asked, their tone urgent. "You are the sole student on record who has seriously explored this layer and returned to tell the tale. Even among the faculty, only a select few have ever ventured into these depths. What was it you saw here?"

Even as the great sage spoke, Walker had his rucksack on the ground, doing stretches. His eyes locked on the view before them.

"I've come back here to make sure of *that*. Can't wait. My heart's singing out loud. I get to tackle this!"

His voice quivered with excitement. This was clearly a dream come true.

Realizing further prodding would get them nowhere, Farquois hung their head. "You've forgotten me entirely. This entire trip was a waste of my time! Fine, so be it. I'm the one who said it wouldn't make me break a sweat."

Abandoning their efforts, Farquois spun on their heel and walked away. Oliver and Guy jumped and turned their way—and a voice came over the great sage's shoulder.

"You've caught your glimpse, boys. Time you got on home. I'll take you as far as the fourth layer—that should be enough, right, Mr. Walker?"

"Yeah, thanks. Sorry I'm like this, Mx. Farquois. We'll have to have a real chat when I return."

Walker's tone had shifted dramatically. He hadn't glanced their way—but this was the first real indication he was actually conscious of the great sage's presence. That caught Farquois by surprise, and they snorted awkwardly.

"I won't pin my hopes too high. But go on, have your fun—do try not to die."

It was hard to tell if that was encouragement or spite; either way, Farquois was already walking back up the cave. Oliver and Guy took a step after them, then looked back once.

"We'll await your safe return, Walker."

"Let's have another first-layer barbeque! I'll make sure the whole gang's there!"

Both meant every word. Walker said nothing more—just shot them a thumbs-up. A sight that made it hard to worry.

Putting their faith in him, the boys turned and set out upon their journey back to the campus above.

All gods worshipped by Gnostics demanded oaths in return, and these colored the lives of their followers, differing them from the norm. To prevent discovery, they were forced into a variety of disguises and subterfuge—but in all such cases, the more followers there were, the harder it was to hide. Blending into ordinary villages, building settlements of their own in the wilderness—in each case, once the population swelled beyond a given point, the approach was no longer practical.

But they were not just given restrictions. In return for those labors, they were granted *miracles*. This made things possible, including a full-scale community escaping the attention not just of ordinaries but mages as well.

The Order of the Sacred Light's subterranean sanctuary. A vast undiscovered underground cavern located beneath the western end of the Union, at the back of which lay the center of their sect's veneration. Over eight thousand worshippers resided in the underground village, their lives supported by any number of miracles the god of Uranische-gar provided. All dwellings were constructed of regular polyhedrons, their countless faces giving the streets the appearance of a beehive rolled out lengthwise. The perfection of this design was guaranteed by their god, and as long as they lived according to the oaths, the worshippers here faced no inconvenience.

"How very uyun uyun."

The sanctuary itself was designed to look down upon the followers' lives—it, too, was built from conjoined polyhedrons. In a room near the top was a seat reserved for those most revered. A girl clad in a pure-white habit sat there, and the whisper that crossed her lips made the man feeding her bread dipped in soup froze.

"...Do you not like it? My apologies."

"No, not the food, Helissio. I mean you. The bread is quite nice. It's extra pwaks pwaks. Did you change the temperature of the kiln?"

The girl smiled. Her eyes had never once opened. Helissio returned the smile, placing a hand to his chest in a show of reverence.

"Thank you," he said. "Our oaths require our food to be simple, but if I can provide any pleasure to you within those terms..."

"Why change the shape and texture daily?" a flat voice cut in.

Helissio looked up to see a bald man clad in the same plain habit that he wore. The bald man's face was devoid of expression, eerily unchanging, like he was molded out of plaster.

His eyes on the tray's food, he moved only his lips, and even then— very slightly.

"Yesterday, it was cut thin. Two days ago, in cubes. Three days ago, there was a vegetable paste smeared on it, and today, you've dunked it in bean soup. What purpose does these alterations serve? Would it not suffice to repeat a unified superior form?"

Helissio grimaced at this and went back to feeding the girl. Tearing off a piece of bread, dunking it in the soup, and carefully conveying it to the girl's mouth.

"I doubt you'd understand. But humans soon grow tired of the same thing. Repetition of anything soon drains the joy from it. Perhaps that merely speaks to our own imperfections."

"Heh-heh, I love all your food, Helissio. I could not possibly pick just one. That one's best, this one's best, they're all the best. Nothing wrong with having many good things."

"Optimal is...plural? A contradiction. I fail to comprehend."

Baffled, the man tilted his head—at far too great an angle for that word to really apply. Like an awkward imitation of a human behavior he'd once been told was an appropriate expression of confusion.

The girl swallowed her bread and spoke again. "You're worried about Kunigunde, Helissio?"

"...Honestly, yes. We've had no contact from her since her infiltration mission began. I'm aware where she is makes communication difficult, but..."

This admission clearly pained him, but his head snapped up, spotting something new. This location was the pinnacle of their settlement and afforded a view of the entirety—he'd spotted one of their own coming down the path on the far-side dwellings, through the passage to the surface.

"Old Evit and Nicolas have returned. I'm sure they'll report in soon."

"I shall go to greet them. Helissio, hold my hand?"

"Happily."

Helissio stood up and obsequiously took the girl's hand. As he led the way, her eyes remained closed, her movements distinctly those of one who could not see. As they moved to the window, the bald man mutely followed, the wall of the sanctuary rebuilding itself into a flowing staircase that led downward from these heights. During their slow descent, they were met by their returning colleagues. One was a tall elder with a long pentagonal staff. The priest, Evit. He knelt before the girl.

"Lady Linnea, you need not have come to me. I would have dragged my old bones to see you soon enough."

"Though the words you speak are true... ♪"

"...They'll make Lady Linnea come to you! ♪"

New faces approached the original group of five. Two singsong voices, but it was hard to say if they belonged to two girls—for they were joined together at the torso. Yet, their feet never faltered, their advance accompanied by an especially large figure. A man with a dog's head, clad in a habit. At a glance, he appeared to be a kobold, but the skeletal structure differed, and the gleam of intelligence in his eyes was far too strong.

"The length of your absence led to this, Evit. Lady Linnea missed you so. Were you not due back five days ago?"

The dogheaded man spoke fluently, though there were no recorded instances of kobolds mastering human speech anywhere in the Union.

"I cannot deny it," Evit said, nodding to him. "Alas, my feet grow slow. Perhaps it's time I retire."

"How many times do I have to tell you not to blame your age? Even if your back was thoroughly bent, you've not the character to desire retirement."

This voice came from the opposite direction, and Evit turned around to find a male elf wearing a similar habit, half his pointy ears missing. As the old man made to respond, the small-statured boy beside him took a hesitant step forward, peering at the girl from a hood pulled down across his eyes.

"...L-Lady Linnea," he stammered. "H-how...fare you?"

His voice was oddly raspy—and at the sound of it, the ground at his feet rusted over. Beneath the hood was a baby face, 80 percent of which was covered in reddish rust, like painful scabs. These went down his neck, suggesting his entire body was in this condition. An uncanny sight, yet—

"Oh!" the girl said, smiling warmly. "Nicolas, you've grown so good at speaking. I do love your voice. It's warm and fyula fyula."

She moved right up to Nicolas, reaching out her hands and brushing his rusty cheeks without concern. The boy closed his eyes, basking in it, and gave a sigh of relief.

"I'm doing great," she said. "I can even hop up and down if I choose. Should I demonstrate?"

"Please don't, Lady Linnea. The last time, you twisted your ankle badly. And you know how hard Nicolas took that."

"Aww, but I'd get it right this time!"

The girl puffed out her cheeks. Helissio winced and took a step forward, gently pulling the boy's hood back. The rust ran up his cheeks and across his head, but Helissio looked upon him as one would a brother.

"You've built up a lot of rust, Nicolas. I'll get you clean soon."

"Th-thank...you," Nicolas said with a bashful smile.

Evit glanced around the assembled faces, then spoke solemnly.

"The time is but a year away. Are we all ready for it?"

The mood shifted immediately. The conjoined girls bared canines, laughing musically. The dogheaded man flexed his grip. The elf with severed ears filled himself with mana. The warm, relaxed mood gone in a flash—each one of them ready for a fight.

"When we need to fight... ♪"

"...You'll find our readiness is right! ♪"

"A foolish question, Evit. We are *always* prepared."

"Any time. Merely waiting for the moment to arrive."

"...Fooo... Fooo...!"

Nicolas quivered bodily, a wheeze escaping his throat, and the rusty corruption at his feet rapidly spread out around him. Joy and suffering mingled on his face, caught in between. As if in response to this emotional outburst, the ground shook.

"WOOOOOOOOOOOOOOOOOOOOOO!!!"

And a tremendous howl echoed far and wide. A massive *something* rose up beside the sanctuary the girl had been. An arm thicker than a tree trunk raised high. Merely shifting the legs on folded knees alone was enough to shake the cavern. Two massive eyes were aglow with a dark light. The worshippers in the dwellings fell to their knees in awe.

And the girl put her arms around Nicolas, holding him tight. The tension drained from him, and the cultists all snapped out of their fervor. The girl patted Nicolas gently on the back, speaking to them all.

"It's too soon to get all bahfoh bahfoh." Her voice as calm as ever, soothing her fellows, then she addressed the giant thing above. "Settle down, Sulfo. You'll hit your head on the ceiling again."

The giant dropped back into the shadow of the sanctuary. The cultists knelt reverentially before the girl; no matter how much power they might have, no one here would go against her word.

"We don't have long to wait. Until the day our god draws near. They'll set the stage for us, I'm sure."

The girl smiled, speaking warmly.

The Oracle, Linnea.

A blind, ordinary girl—and the leader of the Order of the Sacred Light.

Farquois escorted them to the fourth layer, and there, they split up, Oliver and Guy making their own ways home. The great sage watched their students pass through the library tower, then whispered sadly.

"…They're both trying so hard to grow. How adorable, really."

Then they turned, heading back the way they'd come—to the fifth layer. An area infamous for the sheer quantity of dragons, but it had one other distinctive feature. Almost nobody ever went there. A few instructors kept workshops within, although as long as one knew their general locations, it was easy enough to avoid chance encounters.

"This should do," said Farquois. "Ready, Kunigunde?"

Farquois spoke to empty air at the bottom of a canyon. No answer met them. Yet, Farquois smiled as if one had—and they drew their athame.

"Very well. Then come on out."

With that, they sliced open their own side. A gash so deep, their entrails spilled out on the ground before them—but these quickly swelled up, taking human form. In a matter of seconds, there knelt a woman, lightly dressed, drenched in Farquois's blood.

"…Took you…long enough," she managed. "I thought—you were going to make me part of you forever."

"Perish the thought. It was necessary to get around Kimberly security, but I won't do this twice. Turning you into a part of myself to smuggle you in? Simply ghastly."

Farquois was calmly healing the wound shut. The woman stood up, shaking herself off and opening her eyes. They gradually came into focus.

"…At last, my eyes can see again. This means I'm free to begin?"

"Mm. I've learned the lay of the land from the campus through the labyrinth. You should be free to move around. But watch out for students as well as staff. The children here are well trained. Even those in lower forms are not to be trifled with, and many of the older ones are more than a match for you."

"…Heh-heh… This hellscape's reputation proceeds it. How terrified my father must have been, infiltrating this place on his own."

Her voice quivered. Realizing that, she stifled it, recovering herself—and knelt before the great sage again.

"Let us work together, until our desire is met, and our god arrives.

"Rod Farquois. High Priest of the Triangle, blessed by the Sacred Light."

A title they did not often go by—but Farquois merely smiled. The smile of a confident, merciful mage, no different from the one they showed their students.

END

Afterword

Hello, I am Bokuto Uno. Though affairs have settled down for now, the footsteps of coming calamity echo through those halls—as you have seen.

It's grown clear why the Five Rods sent their agent to Kimberly, but Rod Farquois marches to a tune all their own. They suggest they once met Two-Blade, but the specifics are shrouded in mystery. Perhaps their true motives and allegiances will reveal themselves only after the mage takes action.

Thus, curtains fall on the fourth year. Sensing troubles to come, all Kimberly students prepare themselves as best they can. But that goes for the school's enemies as well. If Kimberly is a hell for mages, then the Gnostics approach from the abyss beyond. Loathing and cursing the world that destroyed them, hoping salvation from outside it will change everything.

War is coming. Readers—prepare yourselves.

HAVE YOU BEEN TURNED ON TO LIGHT NOVELS YET?

86—EIGHTY-SIX, VOL. 1-13

In truth, there is no such thing as a bloodless war. Beyond the fortified walls protecting the eighty-five Republic Sectors lies the "nonexistent" Eighty-Sixth Sector. The young men and women of this forsaken land are branded the Eighty-Six and, stripped of their humanity, pilot "unmanned" weapons into battle...

Manga adaptation available now!

WOLF & PARCHMENT, VOL. 1-10

The young man Col dreams of one day joining the holy clergy and departs on a journey from the bathhouse, Spice and Wolf. Winfiel Kingdom's prince has invited him to help correct the sins of the Church. But as his travels begin, Col discovers in his luggage a young girl with a wolf's ears and tail named Myuri, who stowed away for the ride!

Manga adaptation available now!

SOLO LEVELING, VOL. 1-8

E-rank hunter Jinwoo Sung has no money, no talent, and no prospects to speak of—and apparently, no luck, either! When he enters a hidden double dungeon one fateful day, he's abandoned by his party and left to die at the hands of some of the most horrific monsters he's ever encountered.

Comic adaptation available now!